WAYWARD
WESTY

WAYWARD WESTY

Laurence R. McCarthy

Library of Congress Control Number:		2011914728
ISBN:	Hardcover	978-1-4653-0108-6
	Softcover	978-1-4653-0107-9
	Ebook	978-1-4653-0452-0

To order additional copies of this book, contact:
Xlibris Corporation
0800-891-366
www.xlibris.co.nz
Orders@xlibris.co.nz
700138

CONTENTS

CHAPTER ONE.. 7

CHAPTER TWO   Whatapu 28

CHAPTER THREE   The Far North 37

CHAPTER FOUR   A New Beginning 48

CHAPTER FIVE   Oz 71

CHAPTER SIX   Good Ol' Enzed 83

CHAPTER SEVEN   The Straight and Narrow...........89

CHAPTER EIGHT   Veggie Gardens and Bread 99

CHAPTER NINE   What Next? 106

CHAPTER TEN   Back to Oz...................................111

CHAPTER ELEVEN   The West Is the Best 128

CHAPTER TWELVE   Mangonui...................................140

CHAPTER THIRTEEN   Trucks 'n' Boats........................146

CHAPTER FOURTEEN 153

CHAPTER ONE

Larry Matchell, born August 1949, a Leo, or an ox if you take it by the Chinese way of astrology Is the sort of bloke most people get along with. A thick crop of hair and rugged face lets you know he's an adventurous type, with broad shoulders and thick chest, tapered to the waist. His solid legs give the ability to go anywhere they would like to take him.

Larry grew up in a small suburban town in west Auckland, New Zealand. It was the kinda place you really felt in touch with, as in the fifties, New Zealand was just that, about fifty years behind the rest of the world. Hell's teeth, you had to have overseas funds to buy a flamin' car, cost five pence to go to the matinee movies, buy a gobstopper for a flamin' penny, and buy a packet of fags for nine pence.

Brought up by his parents, his ol' man bein' an immigrant cockney, his mum a full-blown Kiwi, life was great! He attended the local primary school, intermediate, and then college, where of course, he met all of his mates. A good bunch of guys all into their sport—soccer, rugby, cricket, not that he had much to do with the latter, though had one game, got bowled for a duck and never bothered goin' back.

He tried his hand at soccer and rugby and was a great achiever in both. One sport he was keen on was tennis only because he could spend hours and hours whackin' the ball against a brick wall.

Bein' a solitary guy, Larry learnt to be on his own due to the fact that he had two sisters. Growin' up with two girls in tow was sometimes a bit of a mission, but that was only for the first seven years when the ol' man and his mom told him he was goin' to have a bro. Christ, that was the best thing ever, a bro!

Life carried on through the fifties, all the things a young fella does he did.

Over the road from the homestead was what all the locals called 'The Gully'. This was basically a swamp shredded with willow trees and a small creek loaded with eels. Larry spent hours and hours pokin' about there with his homemade spear and slingshot. Sometimes his mate next door went there with him, and they'd spend all day dammin' up the creek, till it got to the stage where the bloody creek backed up so much, the dam burst, sending a torrent of water cascading through the gully, wiping out trees, scouring out the banks, and generally just makin' a flamin' big mess.

When he wasn't doin' that, it was eelin'.

'The Gully' must have been a breeding ground for eels as there were literally thousands of elvers there. His mate, a grubby little urchin, always pickin' his arse or nose, covered in school sores, caught these little buggers and ate them alive. Larry tried it once or twice but couldn't hack feeling o' them wriggle down his throat.

If it wasn't muckin' about eeling, it was hut building time, and he did build some awesome huts.

'The Gully' actually backed on to the local horse-racing track. A big bank ran up out of there, which was covered in gorse, this was a great spot to build a hut as it was concealed from the rest of the kids in the neighbourhood. This was really important, as if they found where it was, they would wreck it for sure; besides, it was a good spot to hide all the booty he acquired in his travels, you know, mainly food and of course, the ol' man's tools that he wasn't supposed to have. He got stuck in and started to build the hut of all huts. First of all, he burrowed a big cave out of the side of the bank. This went in about two metres, propping the roof with logs of willow that he had harvested from 'The Gully' and a real hunky-dory willow log lean-to which jutted out from the great hole in the bank. This hut was the best thing since sliced bread.

Larry kept it a secret for a good two months until he raced over there one day after school only to discover someone had found his hideaway. He was devastated; whoever had found it had turfed out his booty and loaded up with their own stash. Larry couldn't believe it: axes, torches, saws, electric drills, hammers, and a whole lot of other items of hardware. 'Who the, what the hell's goin' on?'. This was a real bonus; the only thing that was worrying him was 'who was it?'

The next weekend, Larry staged a stake out. He sat and waited, but no one turned up, so he crept back into his precious hut. It wouldn't have been five minutes when bugger me if the bloke across the road showed up. It was Joseph. He poked his head through the doorway and asked what he was doing there.

Joe was about four years elder than Larry, tight curly hair, broad shoulders, muscles all over him—a daunting sight to a nine-year-old. Larry explained that it was his hut, but if Joe wanted to use it, that was OK! Joe agreed, but made it quite clear that he was to tell not a sole!

Joe was a petty thief raiding all the local shops with his mate, a Pakeha bloke from the other side of the racecourse. He wasn't the sort of bloke you would wanna mess with. Hell's teeth he was strollin' up the street one Sunday arvo with a slug pistol in his hand poppin' off the ceramic power connectors on the power poles, birds, anything he fancied, even to the extent that he shot poor ol' Dave, Larry's next door neighbour, right between the eyes, didn't give a shit. Not being a particularly high-powered pistol, the slug didn't penetrate his scull but just buried itself into the skin, looking like a big blackhead. A proper arsehole!

His brother Steve was a good bloke, though, into hunting, in fact, he was a culler for the government and was always away on expeditions down country after the feral deer, pigs, and goats. When Steve was home, however, he kept Joe well in tow being the eldest of all, and man, he gave him a hiding.

Yep, life was great all right goin' to school, comin' home, havin' a feed and rushin' over the road to the hut to see if there were any more goodies.

Larry thought to himself one day, 'What the hell am I doin' with my life? Here I am, an eleven-year-old, bloody bored'. He decided it was about time he made a change, playing around with huts, and shootin' his slingshot was not really something he was entirely happy with, but then again the slingshot had its moments, especially shootin' bottles from the swing he had erected.

This massive single rope swing hung from the biggest willow tree you would ever hope to see.

Fortunately, it just happened to be growing in just the right spot, about eight or nine metres out from the Gullie's bank. Larry clambered up the tree and fixed the rope to the highest point possible, and attached to the other end was a piece of wood about two feet long.

He assembled a row of empty beer bottles about thirty feet out past the tree. The idea was to climb up the bank as far as the rope would allow, leap on to the swing with legs either side of the rope, drop your arse down on to the piece of wood, swing out with slingshot in hand, and shoot at the bottles.

A whole crowd of the local neighbourhood blokes gathered there on a regular basis and competition time was on. The bloke who could knock out the most bottles in one swing was the champ. Because this swing was so high, it made the length around the twenty-metre mark, giving the actual swing time quite lengthy, allowing enough time to get off two or three shots throughout the length of the swing. Sometimes, if you had a good shot it was possible to get two bottles at once.

The Maori jokers from behind Larry's house were good at it, sometimes scooping the pool, but Larry turned out to be the 'King of the Swing'.

The Maoris from over the back were a good bunch. Larry's mum and dad were quite fond of them. One of the boys was a good guitar player and spent hours and hours, teaching Larry the cords 'til eventually he became a rather accomplished player knockin' out the odd Elvis number, but his favourite was Country music.

The two of them sat out in the tool shed in the backyard and yodelled away nearly every Sunday arvo. Johno and Larry became quite good mates, with Larry looking up to Johno being the eldest an' all.

Johno's elder bro, Frank, was the real quiet mysterious type, a well built, strong as an ox Maori fella. Ever since he was a boy, he'd always wanted to be in the army, and he paraded around as if he was playin' war all by himself.

Early one morning, Larry's ol' man got up for work, he was huntin' about the house for his work shoes, he could have sworn he'd left them in the kitchen foyer, no not there, even his best shoes were gone from the dining room. 'What the hell is going on here?' he coulda sworn!

Anyway, Larry had built a new hut, this time really secluded over in the scrub alongside the racecourse. He had wandered over there one afternoon to find to his astonishment all the ol' man's shoes in his hut. He couldn't believe it; some bastard had found his hut, flogged stuff from his ol' man, not only his shoes but a whole lot of paint, paint brushes, tools, and a whole array of things from out of the ol' man's garage.

The blood ran out of Larry's face as he thought of the rage when his dad found out. When he broke the news, he was right! His ol' man went into an uproar.

'That bloody arsehole thievin' bastard!' That flogged his gear he was goin' to 'break his bloody neck' if he found out who it was.

Over the next couple of weeks, Larry kept a close watch over his hut, but no one came near it until one morning he could hear his ol' man roarin' his head off out in his garage. The same thief had ripped off his paint that he was to use on a job he was to do that day, and bein' a painter and decorator, the paint was a special mix.

Larry shot out to where his hut was and bugger me dead, there was Frank just comin' out of it. Larry ducked down behind some bushes as if Frank had seen him; he would more than likely give him a hiding.

'Shit!' He thought to wait till the ol' man found out. Larry thought of what he would say to Frank as Frank was a big bastard. Larry broke the news to his dad, with his dad lettin' him know he would handle it. His dad marched next door to see Frank's ol' man. Him and Larry's ol' man got on good together as they were both returned soldiers from the Second World War and hard as nails. It later worked with Frank having to apologise to the ol' man and return all the booty.

Frank sauntered off up to Larry's hut to collect it all. When he came back, Larry's ol' man asked where the rest of the paint was. Frank insisted that 'that was all there was' and of course, Larry's ol' man knew different, but he couldn't prove it, he let the matter go.

About six months later, on a beautiful sunny day, Frank came over to ask if they could loan his trestles. They were going to paint their house and of course, he said yes.

After a bit of pottering in his garage, Larry's dad was hailed for lunch.

Tom was hesitant over lunch and couldn't help but think about the neighbour's paintin' their house, he couldn't take it any more, raced outside, and to the next door he flew. 'Bloody arseholes', he yelled. They were painting their house with the paint he had mixed for the special job he was to do six months ago. He grabbed his trestles, vowing never to do anything for them ever again, but of course, he did, after he had cooled down.

Larry had a lot to do with the neighbours and as he got elder, it was the girls that took his fancy, especially Laura from down the road. Laura was a quiet gentle girl. Her auburn hair fell gently on to her shoulders, framing her youthful thirteen-year-old face, with deep brown eyes softening her whole being.

Laura was a mature young lass with rather large and protruding breasts and an hourglass figure. Larry was always a bit smitten of Laura and as he was getting elder, certain feelings, especially in the groin department came to fore.

One sunny Saturday arvo Larry bumped into Laura strollin' past his house. After a bit of a chat, Larry persuaded her to come over to 'The Gully' for a bit of an explore, all the time wondering how he was goin' to swoon her. After a bit of a play around, Larry eventually got what he was after. There she was lying on a bed of soft green grass, her dress up around her waist, and her knickers neatly folded beside her. Larry couldn't believe it; she looked so beautiful, his knees were trembling. Not only his knees but his whole body was in such a state of excitement, fear, trauma that he could hardly get his pants down, panicking every time he looked down at her little patch of hair.

His penis was so hard it hurt.

All of a sudden, somethin' turned off the lights as he heard this deep manly voice behind him. Christ Almighty! It was the deer culler, Steve. Bloody Larry shit himself, what the fuck now! Laura was scramblin' about in one hell of a panic. Steve obviously wanted a piece of the pie and wasted no time. Steve was nineteen and had a cock on him like a donkey; well, that's what it appeared like to the two young innocent thirteen—and fourteen—year-olds who didn't know what the fuck to do.

All Larry could do was watch as this mongrel, whom he admired and looked up to growing up, pin Laura to the ground and rape her. He was so traumatised by it all he was numb all over. Tears were streaming down Laura's face, blood all over the grass.

Steve pulled on his pants and just strolled off into the willows. Larry, still stunned by the whole scene, turned and raced after Steve pickin' up a big hunk o' wood on the way. He screamed up behind him, lifting the hunk o' wood, ready to whack the bastard over the head when all of a sudden, Steve swung around just in time to see what was happenin' and stepped aside. Larry anticipated this and swung the other way catchin'

Steve on the side of his face. He went down like a pole-axed bull, blood pissin' outta his nose and ear.

Steve lay there motionless with Larry standin' over him. Larry was tremblin' so much he could hardly stand on his own two feet. The whole world was flashin' through his head; he knew that Steve was goin' to be OK as he was lettin' out a bit of a moan.

'Stuff me dead this arseholes goin' to finish me off when he comes to', he thought, 'what the hell I am goin' to do!' Larry turned to help Laura. She was just sitting there, sobbing.

Larry went over to her to comfort her; she put her arms around him so tight Larry thought she would never let go.

He lifted her to her feet, gathering up his pants and slippin' them on. Steve was just startin' to stir when they passed him by, his face buried in the mud of the swamp.

They quickly ran up and out of 'The Gully' and on to the road. They both agreed to keep the whole thing quiet, fearing the repercussions from their parents, unless Steve bashed him up; then they agreed to spill the beans.

Weeks went by and not a word was mentioned about the whole affair. Larry hardly leaving his home except to go to school. He saw Laura a few times after everything had simmered down, but the bond between them slowly dwindled. Larry knew this would affect her for the rest of her life.

The months ticked over, Larry got stuck into his sport: soccer, rugby, tennis. He was a number eight in rugby, being the last man down in the scrum. Larry wasn't all that keen on rugby as he thought the game really didn't give you a lot of time to think and enjoyed the soccer better as it stimulated him to the brink of excitement at every confrontation.

Although Larry played at centre half, he got to take most of the corner kicks and I tell you, talk about 'Bend It like Beckham', he could curl the ball so well that nine times out of ten he would score. The opposition didn't have a clue that this would happen and were most of the time caught off guard.

Larry went on to be an Auckland City Representative and of course, his ol' man Tom, bein' a pom and all, was really chuffed. His parents got involved with his club and were always supportive, attending most of the socials and events.

These social events started to become an issue with his parents as ol' Tom hit the piss and his mum, Vivian, was embarrassed by it all.

They held numerous parties at home also, and it was always Tom that had to be picked up off the floor or chastised for lewd acts.

The booze was starting to become a major problem between them with Tom's attendance at the local Returned Serviceman's Club, or RSA for short, being a thorn in the side to Viv. Tom's drinking got worse and worse to the stage where he was hiding bottles of plonk in the hall cupboard, bottles of whisky in the toilet cistern, crates of beer in the garage, just becomin' a bloody nightmare for the whole family.

It became embarrassing for Larry's sisters also as he got pissed and became suggestive towards their friends whenever they came and slept over. Viv had a friend over the shore she'd go stay with for a break but that became a hassle also so she stopped that.

Larry was nearing manhood at fourteen and with his parents the way they were affected his schooling and inevitably started to run off the rails, waggin' school, fightin', smokin', girlin' especially the twins from next door.

Hell's teeth all he had to do was snap his fingers, and their knickers would fall to the ground. Larry screwed the fuck out of those two whenever he felt like it; in fact, a lot of girls fancied him as he was growing up to be a real 'Don Juan'.

Larry's mum started a job in a factory as a short order cook. This was fantastic for her as she met a lot of friends there.

One friend in particular turned out to be a man! The relationship was purely platonic in the beginning, but things started to escalate. When Larry and his sisters found out about it, they laughed like hell, not that they thought it was a bad thing, but it was when their mum told them his name, Rupert, they cracked up. It was all hush hush, of course, but the kids thought if it was givin' their mum happiness, so be it.

Rupert was an inoffensive bloke who liked to go dancing, wasn't a big drinker, which to Viv meant a lot, especially after booze and abuse. They met secretly at her friend's house and went out dancin' and having a great time while ol' Tom just kept on drinkin' his life away.

The situation was gradually coming to a head-on at the home front. Larry's eldest sis met a chap who was twelve years her senior and fell in love, or so she thought, and wanted to marry him and take off back to Italy where he was from. Of course, Tom was outraged, stating that he used to fight against those buggers during the war and no daughter of his was going to marry the enemy! But he was outvoted, and she did get married, and they took off to Oz from Whenuapai on the Lockheed Electra turbo prop plane. She was only seventeen.

Larry always had a special spot for his ol' man, and he really felt for him seeing his daughter flyin' off to the other side of the world with the enemy. He had to come to terms with the fact the world moves on, even in the sixties.

Larry's youngest sis became somewhat a renegade, knockin' about with all the riff-raff around town, eventually ending up bein' expelled from school. With all this happenin' around them, Larry's mum and dad eventually split up.

Larry's bro was too young really to understand what was goin' on. The house went on the market was sold, and the money split two ways. They both ended up with seventeen hundred and fifty pounds each, A lot of dough those days.

Larry went with his dad; it was his decision entirely, his sis and young bro goin' with Viv. The only thing that cut the ol' man up was the fact that Viv had moved in with Rupert. When he had eventually found out about the affair, he hit the piss even more and was continually drunk.

Viv had a rented house in the bush out at Titirangi, a big ol' brick joint up on a hill which she and Rupert moved half the furniture into. Larry was left to move him and Tom into a flat, a flat roofed pad in a block of three on the other side of the racecourse. Tom was so pissed the day they moved that Larry had to get a helpin' hand from neighbours.

Sheila, who was one o' the Maoris from over the back fence, and her husband offered a hand. Pete was a merchant seaman and a bloody neat bloke, not only that but he had an F100 pickup truck, which Larry drooled over. They loaded up and moved all the gear into the flat, having to look after Tom at the same time, as by that stage, he was legless.

Everybody settled in, with Larry goin' to school only occasionally. All he wanted to do was finish his schooling and get into work.

It was the year that he was to sit his school certificate exams but there was no way he was even interested.

Life at home wasn't all that great. His ol' man was still goin' to work but gettin' on the piss every night to the stage where he wrote himself off, Larry havin' to sit there and listen to him rattle out all these war songs till he flaked.

Tom always carried heaps of cash on him and half the time he was oblivious to the fact that he was loose and half of it droppin' out of his pockets.

He threw the occasional party with a whole heap o' blokes frontin' up from the RSA or pub.

It was OK. Larry always sneaked a few beers and often took the opportunity to make the most of it by invitin' some of his mates along. He became attached to a young bloke next door who was in his twenties.

Trev was a likeable chap, tall and skinny, with long straggly greasy hair, little narrow shoulders, long sinewy arms covered in tatts and hands like giant—sized rump steaks.

Trev was not the skinny pune that he appeared to be. He was never outta jeans and was always covered in grease from workin' on his 46 Ford Mercury.

Every now and again, he asked Larry if he would like to go for a spin with him, mainly to pick up a few parts. Now and again, he brought his young two-year-old son with them to give his pretty wife, Sophie, a break. This was a welcomed treat for Larry as he dearly missed the comfort of his family life that he had once had. Trev and Sophie sometimes popped over for a few drinks; he wanted to keep an eye on things just to make sure nothin' untoward happened. He kinda took Larry under his wing in a way as he had fathomed out that if there was any trouble, he was on hand to deal with it, with Larry's ol' man bein' the way he was he wouldn't have much of a show if any trouble brewed.

Eventually, Trev's hunch paid off. One Saturday night, Tom had a couple o' mates around for a few. Everything was cotia with the ol' radiogram bashin' out some good ol' fifties numbers with a bit of Vera Lynn thrown in to satisfy some o' the ol' war boys.

Tom for once wasn't as pissed as he usually was and everyone was havin' a ball. Larry was chattin' away to a couple o' sheilas in the kitchen, and Trev was yakkin' away to a couple of blokes who had tagged along from the pub.

Larry could hear his ol' man raising his voice, tellin' someone to fuck off outta there. He poked his head into the lounge; there were a couple of jokers in there who weren't there before. Tom shoutin' at them both. They were gate crashers that had got wind of a party happenin' at Tom's place and weren't welcome as they were known troublemakers.

Things started to heat up with one of them shovin' Tom, causing him to fall over backwards hittin' his head on the corner of the lounge suite. Well, if you had ever seen a snake strike, this was even faster. Trev was across the room and landed a bunch o' fives on this dude with such force that it smacked him from one side o' the room to the other; it was all on. He got himself together and charged at Trev.

This dude was a whoppa, comin' across the room like a pit bull in a dogfight; he took a swing at Trev, which copped him on his shoulder. Trev faltered for a tick and ducked just in time as this scrapper threw another, just as well because if that had landed Trev would have been a gonna for sure. Trev came back and under and collected this bloke with a crushing blow just under his nose, causing blood to spurt out over the carpet.

The pit bull charged at Trev, grapplin' with him on the floor, both exchangin' blow for blow. Trev was underneath him but managed a Liverpool kiss fair on the snoz. He reeled back, Trev leapin' to his feet in an instant charging at him like a hyped up foxy at the same time throwin' the final blow, fair on the chin the pit bull droppin' to the ground out cold. Larry and everyone else keepin' outta the way whenever they could. Some of the sheilas were bowled over, furniture was everywhere.

The pit bull's mate started to make a move towards Trev but didn't have a shit show as before ya knew it a couple of the ol' digger mates of Tom had him wrapped up before he had a chance to say 'Jack Robinson'. What a scrap! Larry had seen his ol' man in action in the past when he beat up the neighbour for bashin' his kids up and down their hallway one night, but never a scrap like this.

The two troublemakers were arseholed out and the rest of the night was analysis night with everyone goin' over all the fine points of the fight and of course, Trev was a hero. The next mornin', whoever stayed the night got up and helped clean-up. Tom asked if anyone had found a twenty-quid note, but no one had, he had lost it, probably at the pub.

The boys all started back on the piss at about 10 a.m. They drank all day until really pissed off wives started turnin' up to take them home.

Ah yes, it was a great weekend, all right. Larry thought about the scrap for weeks afterwards and kept thinking of how proud he was of ol' Tom, the fact that he had been sober for once and handled the situation.

Larry had a lot of good memories with his dad. Lookin' back, he was always there for his sport, poppin' along Saturdays to watch him perform, yellin' out from the sideline; in fact, ol' Tom played soccer for the army during the war so when he was asked to play a game for Larry's club, a social one of course, he jumped at the chance. It was a big occasion with ol' Tom gettin' the hype for the big day.

Ol' Tom was a nuggety bloke, of solid build and with short muscly legs. He played mainly in the backs when in the army, but on this day the bloody fools put him out on the left wing, and he was right footed, anyway the whistle went and the game was on, with the other team scoring first. That was OK, but the opposition clicked on to the fact that ol' Tom was out of his league on the wing and continually feed the ball out to the left. This was really gettin' the hackles on Tom's back to stick up as the bloke he was markin' was a tall, long-legged, fast bastard.

The ball shot out to the wing once again with this lanky bugger flyin' down towards ol' Tom. Here he was runnin' like fuck after this bloke got right up behind him, but just couldn't quite catch him, so he did a flyin' leap forward and tackled him, grabbin' him around the legs in a perfect rugby-styled fashion, bringing him to the ground like a 'slam dunk!' Well, there was an uproar. The bloke got up off the ground and charged at ol' Tom, but Tom had somethin' else up his sleeve. What they all didn't know was that Tom, before the war, was an expert wrestler, and just grabbed this bloke and had him tied up in seconds. The whole field ran over to the ruckus, all pushin' and shovin', Ol' Tom hopped up off the ground and just stood there, watchin' it all.

Later on in the club rooms, after they had all had a few, the whole bunch o' 'em couldn't stop laughin' about it as they all saw the funny side everyone pattin' ol' Tom on the back, lettin' him know they all approved. They all knew that Tom was out-classed on the wing and that was the only way he could finally stop his opposition.

Not only soccer but other sport Tom backed Larry with. He joined them both up in a small bore rifle club when Larry was only ten. Well, you would think all Larry's Christmases had come at once.

Tom was never that keen on rifles, probably because of the war, but Larry Excelled, becomin' one of the best shots there, over and above the big boys. Tom was proud of him.

Not only in the sport that they were together, but Tom and Larry often went away campin' for the long weekends. One particular trip was up north. Tom and Larry loaded up the family Humber Hawk and headed off with well wishes from Viv and the kids. Cruisin' along in the country side, Larry spotted a pheasant feedin' away in a paddock and beckoned his dad to go back and have a pop at it with the twenty-two.

Tom hove too and put the ol' Humber in reverse and snuck back to where Larry had seen the pheasant. There it was, about thirty yards away.

Tom took the rifle out of the backseat, slipped the bolt into place, poked it out the window, slid a round up the spout, and took aim.

To Larry, it seemed like an eternity before Tom pulled the trigger, all the while Larry thinkin' he can't miss, and he did! Unbelievable! Then again, when Larry grew elder, he realised that ol' Tom probably missed for a reason and that would have been because of the war.

Larry understood that Tom was sick to death of killing. They carried on their way and eventually arrived at the most beautiful bay you would ever hope to see. Tom had to get permission to pass through a farm to the beach where the paddocks were halted by gently sloping cliffs, festooned with the native Pohutukawa trees, and down on to the white sandy beach below.

Tom drove down to a spot by a ramblin' brook that spilled out on to the beach. Larry could hardly wait to get to explore the place. Tom pulled up the ol' Humber by the stream, where it was flat enough to pitch the pup tent and proceeded to unload the gear. The two of them put up the tent, stashed the gear, and then took off down to the beach. There wasn't a sole in sight as they gazed out over the sea towards a small island the locals called 'Goat Iland'.

The sea was flat, calm, with the afternoon sun dancing on the surface.

Larry, being adventurous as he was, tootled off round the rocks while Tom headed back to the camp site to prepare dinner.

After rock hoppin' for about ten minutes, Larry stumbled over a large rock pool about ten or maybe fifteen yards in diameter. He gazed down into the crystal waters and to his surprise, the pool was at least twelve to fourteen feet deep. He could make out movement down in the depths, and the harder he looked, he realised it was chocker block with fish.

That night Larry and ol' Tom chatted away about huntin' and fishin', eventually hittin' the sack about midnight. Larry had a restless sleep dreamin' about the pool.

He leapt out of bed at sparrow's fart, keen to get down to the beach.

Tom was already up and had breaky half-cooked bacon and eggs, what else! Whilst Larry had been explorin', Tom was busy gettin' his fishin' gear ready and was all prepared for the day ahead.

Larry was a little keen on snorkelling, so he had his mask, snorkel, and flippers all ready to get goin'. The two of them wafted down their tucker, then headed down to the beach, and made their way towards the pool, Larry striding ahead of his father in haste to get there.

By the time Tom arrived, Larry was already in the drink, gazing down into the pool. There were fish everywhere, of all different shapes and sizes. Larry was aghast with awe as he just hung on the surface taking it all in, then decided to dive. He took a deep breath and down he went, fish darting in all directions as he swam deeper until he was on the bottom.

There were angel fish, Demoiselle, red moki, porae and a whole array of smaller fish dartin' in all directions, when out of the corner of his eye, Larry spotted a couple of whoppers. 'Shit, what is that?' he thought, runnin' out of breath and making to the surface.

Ol' Tom had organised his fishin' spot and had his line in the water gettin' a few bites. Larry ran over to him, jaws flappin' like crazy, lettin' him know of the monster fish he had seen.

Tom and Larry mucked about there for most of the mornin', Tom hookin' up a couple o' nice snapper for dinner, when to their surprise they spotted a couple of blokes hoppin' across the rocks towards them. It was Larry's bloody school teacher, Mr Martin, bugger me days, he was gobsmacked. They had a heap of diving gear with them. Larry didn't know he was a diver!

Larry hailed him over, and all the usual greetings took place, with Mr Martin offering to give Larry a demo with a speargun. Crikey dick! Larry had never seen anything like it. It was like a giant rifle, with a stock and a butt, two ginormous rubbers that had to be pulled back to the trigger mechanism, far too powerful for Larry to operate, but that didn't matter as Mr Martin did it for him.

They entered the pool after Larry had described these fish he had seen.

They turned out to be a few snapper that had got trapped in there from the high tide. Mr Martin dived down, stalked one of them and, whammo, shot it! Larry, watchin' the whole ordeal from the surface, said, 'Unbelievable!'

That weekend was Larry's first real introduction to spearfishin', and he loved it and thought to himself it wouldn't be the last. Larry always remembered that weekend with his dad, one of many happy times they spent together.

There were other holidays they had, especially the whole family. One particular one was when they all took off up north on a two-week vacation to a little seaside township on the east coast called 'Whananaki'. It was one of the most favoured spots in New Zealand for a holiday.

A beautiful ocean beach swept around like the new moon stopping at one end at an estuary which oozed into a small inner harbour, abundant with pipis, cockles, flounder, and various other types of seafood. From the estuary, a rocky headland jutted out into the blue Pacific, with cattle grazing on the farmland which covered the top.

Larry's mum and dad had rented a batch for the duration of their stay, a typical 'Kiwi Batch' which was just up the dusty metal road from the local wharf. Of course, Larry and ol' Tom were down there most of the time fishin', and on one particular day, there was all the action.

Tom had his cord fishing line, which had a massive lead weight on the end of it. He unravelled it on to the wharf, grabbed the line about six feet from the end, swung about his head and let it go. Out it flew, about fifty yards and, splash, into the water. Larry's job was to catch the small fry for bait, which consisted mainly of sprats, the best bait you could get.

It was just dawn when they arrived, the early morning mist just starting to disperse. A few big game boats were dotted about the estuary just off the wharf, all facing out to sea on their anchors, indicating that the tide was on its way in.

Larry was busy hanging over the edge off the wharf concentrating on Hookin' up the small fry, when bugger me, he leapt to his feet yellin' at Tom that he had spotted a monster fish swimmin' around the wharf.

Tom came beltin' over to where Larry had seen the fish and sure enough, a bloody great 'kingi'.

Tom raced back to his line at the same time, beckoning to Larry to catch him a 'livey' as the only way to catch a 'Kingi' was with a live bait. Tom attached a freshly caught sprat, took the sinker off, and cast it out, at the same time yellin' out to a woman on one of the big game boats, who was roused by all the yellin' Larry was doin', that there was a big 'Kingi' cruisin' about.

It didn't take her long to duck below deck, and up again, clutchin' the mother of all fishin' rods. It had the biggest reel on it that Larry had ever seen. She cast out a whoppin' big spinner and started to wind it in, as if trolling behind the boat.

She did this several times until, bang! it was on. The reel screamed out at about a hundred miles an hour with this woman holdin' on for dear life. She was yellin' at the top of her voice, indicating that it must be at least an eighty pounder, when the bloody thing turned.

The woman started to take up the slack goin' like hell tryin' to keep the pressure on the line, when finally the line became taught as the monster 'Kingi' started to head for the wharf, the woman pullin' as hard as she could to try and turn the fish.

It finally turned and made its way straight towards the boat, then barrelled out into the direction of the ocean, goin' that fast, the woman just could not hang on and snap! It was all over.

Ol' Tom stood on the wharf, lifeless, whispering to himself 'How the hell couldn't she get that bastard with all that fancy gear!' Then he bent down to pick up his line that was tied to the wharf.

Larry walked over to his dad, feeling sympathetic towards him as he knew that would have fulfilled all his dreams if he had hooked up on that monster fish.

The rest of the holiday was just an awesome experience for the whole Family. Viv bein' right in her element doin' the cookin', walks on the beach with Tom, havin' the family around. The barbeques on the beach were the best that Larry recalled, especially at another beach they had discovered just over the hill.

The fifties in New Zealand was like goin' back in time, as most places were relatively deserted and this particular outta the way place, was just that.

This little, hunky-dory beach was just absolute paradise, Pohutukawa trees dominating the beach front, with small out crops of rocks scattered along the foreshore, pure white sand—a perfect spot for a barbeque.

Tom, Larry, and Larry's elder sis, Katrina, gathered up some driftwood, whilst Viv prepared the food and tendered to Larry's youngest sis, Bobby. Ol' Tom had bought along a piece of old tin to use as a hot plate. Tom fired up the driftwood, and they all sat down to a hearty meal of sausages, steak, big hunks o' bread, and cordial drinks.

It was a great holiday, all right, apart from one incident that frightened the crap out of even ol' Tom. To obtain the milk for the family, Tom had cracked up a deal with the local farmer, whereas he could hop up the road from their batch to the farm's milkin' shed and grab a billy full of fresh cows' milk out of the cool room. Tom had organised with the farmer he'd leave a billy there and fill it for him ready to be picked up. Well, the first day, Larry and Tom headed off up the dusty road towards the milking shed.

It was a good twenty minutes away, with Tom and Larry gasbaggin' about what they were goin' to get up to over the next couple of weeks. They arrived at the farm and slowly sauntered up the drive towards the cowshed, they had only a few yards to go when this bloody cattle dog raced out from under the cream can stand and bailed them both up. It was a Border Collie and, shit, was it vicious. Bloody lips curled right back showing bloody great fangs, back arched up, and growlin' the most menacing growl you've ever heard.

Tom and Larry just froze on the spot with nowhere to run.

If they'd shown any signs of fleeing, this bloody mongrel would have been on them in a flash.

They stood there for a good ten minutes, the dog holdin' its ground with no signs o' lettin' up. Tom noticed a hunk o' wood lyin' on the ground about four or five feet away, but every time he made a move, the bloody dog advanced a little closer with even more vengeance.

Finally, he managed to edge over towards the piece o' wood until he could reach it with his foot, and while he dog dropped its guard for a split second, it was just enough time for Tom to swoop down and pick it up.

The dog saw this and lunged forward in another threatening manner, but Tom showed no fear and stood his ground. He was more concerned about Larry bein' bitten than anything: a father protecting his son!

After a good fifteen minutes, the dog decided that maybe it wasn't a good idea and started to back off much to Tom and Larry's relief. They carried on, picked up the milk, and got the hell outta there.

Later that day, Tom bumped into the farmer as he tootled down the road on his tractor, explained what had happened to him, with the farmer being most apologetic, expressing the fact that they were lucky the bloody dog didn't bite them, as it had happened in the past.

Larry kept up with his schooling, reluctantly, until he had finished his school cert, at least. This was becoming a real pain in the butt.

Larry couldn't concentrate on a bloody thing, what with all the shit goin' down on the home front, it was no wonder. He went to school only just, with the rest of the time waggin', and cruisin' at home.

A couple of sheilas Larry knew, popped in from time to time, for a ciggy and a couple o' drinks, if ol' Tom had any in the fridge.

Of course, when Tom got home, Larry copt it 'big time'. However, these sheilas were quite hot, and after a few days' of smokin' and drinkin', it was smokin', drinkin', and screwin' all day. The school cert. exams were basically put on the back-burner for Larry, as hittin' the piss and screwin' at fifteen-year-old was a bloody sight betterin' school work.

One day, while Larry was waggin' at home, he heard a noise at the door. Larry freaked, as he wasn't aware of any visitors. He peeped out the window, but couldn't see anything, when all of a sudden, the door opened, and who do ya think was standin' there, but Larry's li'l sis, Bobby.

Larry tore over to her and gave her a big hug as Larry and Bobby had always been close as brother and sister. Being only two years between them, they had become even closer since the family bust up. Katrina was in Italy by this time, and young James was only seven. Bobby had got sick of livin' with Viv and Rupert and informed Larry she was there to stay.

Bobby was somewhat, a bit of a rebel, a tomboy, a renegade, and pretty hard to handle, obviously too hard for Viv and Rupert.

There wasn't a school around that could tie her down and, consequently, paid its toll on them both; even though they tried to persuade her to stay, it was like beatin' their head against a brick wall.

Upon seein' Bobby again, it reminded Larry of the things the two of them got up to before the bust up, cruisin' the streets on a Friday or Saturday night, hangin out with their mates, smokin' and drinkin' if they could get their hands on any.

One night Larry and Bobby went cruisin'. There was a sheila whom Bobby knew, who lived in an old hotel up in the township. She had a vendetta on her and was gonna give her a hiding if it killed her.

On this particular night, Larry had managed to get hold of the ol' Humber.

The two of them were drivin' by the hotel when Bobby yelled for Larry to stop! She had spotted this bird just goin' into the front door of the hotel.

Larry screeched to a halt just in time to see Bobby's back as she flew through the front door, makin' a beeline for this sheila. Well, Bobby had grabbed her as she ran up the stairs to the next floor, and all Larry could hear was a lot of screamin' and yellin', a few slaps and thuds, and next thing, Bobby, strollin' out the door with the most satisfied look on her face, stating how she had dealt with her enemy!

After a good ol' chinwag, Bobby and Larry sorted out some digs for Bobby and she settled in for the duration. They both went to school now and again but spent most of the time at home partying up, with, of course, a few mates around. Everything was cruisin' along wonderfully until one day, when Larry was home, doin' a bit of ahem, study, Bobby turned up around 10 a.m. with one of her mates. They couldn't be buggerd with school, so decided home was it, not that Larry minded as her mate was a spunk.

Just as Larry thought things were goin' in his favour, there was a knock on the door. Bobby's mate could see who it was, and it wasn't good. It was the headmistress from school. Larry answered the door to a barrage of questions as to the whereabouts of Bobby and her mate, of course denying he had seen hide nor hair of them, but this didn't deter this dragon by any means, and she barged past Larry and into the flat, mumblin' the whole time that she knew they were there.

She went into all the rooms, but bugger me, they had gone. Larry stood there scratchin' his head after the headmistress had left, when he heard a whimper comin' from the ceiling. He went to the bedroom where the sound was the loudest, tracked the sound to the wardrobe, opened it up, but they were not there; he looked up to a manhole panel in the ceiling, pushed it open, and there they were, just about beside themselves with laughter, and of course, when Larry showed his face, they couldn't hold on any longer and just let rip in raucous laughin' convulsions. Larry saw the funny side, and the three of them laughed for a good ten minutes before settling down to a fag and a beer.

Bobby didn't get away with it, though, and at the end of the day, the system won, and Bobby was expelled; this time being number one.

Tom was rather pleased that Bobby was there with him, but then again he didn't care that much as he was still gettin' his head around the separation from Viv. He got her settled into another school, but sending her to a girls' school couldn't keep Bobby down. Even another school after that, couldn't hold her down, and as she was nearly old enough to leave, anyway, Tom took her out of school and ended up coming up against the welfare system. Poor Bobby had to go back and stay with Viv. Just as well anyway, as Viv was the best of the best mum any son or daughter could hope for.

Even though things weren't that hot between her and Tom, she never let her guard down when it came to her kids.

Larry remembered the home-baked cookies Viv made, and on returning home from school, Viv had put aside the ones that were a little overdone.

They were Larry's favourites, and in fact, the more burnt they were, the better he liked 'em. Some days he would get lucky and end up with half a dozen or more. Viv could never figure out why he liked burnt cookies.

Viv was a beautiful woman who always smelt like a rose, the most caring person one would hope to be acquainted with. She was the sort of a woman whom anyone could depend on, no matter what the situation. Whether it be an errand for someone or caring for the sick, Viv was always there to lend a helping hand.

Viv was also heavily involved with Larry's sport, being on the committee at Larry's footy club, organising functions and balls. She also made a lot of friends, and when all these women got together, it was fun and laughter between them all, crackin' jokes and generally havin' a ball.

Viv was also a competent seamstress and often knocked up a dress or a frock for the girls when they needed them, mainly if it was for a school ball, or as they got elder, especially Katrina, when she had a date.

The best moments for Larry was when he was sick, as Viv was the best nurse on the planet, making sure he felt warm and comfortable, and when he was really down and out, Viv sang lullabies to soothe him as he went off to sleep. Viv was truly a great mum.

The early days of Tom and Viv's marriage were a time to remember for them both, tinkering about in the garden in the weekends, poppin' away on holidays, partying up large at the RSA, they even built their own home, living in a caravan until it was complete. Their marriage only started to deteriorate when stalemate set in, and they started to drift apart.

A few months passed by, and Larry completed his school cert. exams, not that he did any good as all he could think about was work and women.

Tom got booted out of the flat because of all the parties he had and not only that, but the other two flats had young families in them, so they headed out of the area and down to Onehunga. It wasn't a bad pad, in a block of four that was OK as the other tenants were all basically the same sort of people, you know, parties, boozin', and so on.

Tom was still involved in his job as a painter and decorator, but after workin' for himself for the past twelve years or so, it was hard for him to adjust to workin' on wages.

Larry scored a job with Tom's boss, bein' quite a competent painter from the years of holiday work with his dad and all.

Viv had given Larry eighty pounds for a 1937 V8 coupé, which he had had his eyes on at the local car yard. It was a real humdinger. The previous owner had customised it and was now a hot rod, with 100E prefect headlights, a scoop in the bonnet, and VW tail lights. It had a real crackling V8 sound from the twin straight, copper pipes, which protruded from the rear on both sides. This Ford was Larry's second car, the first bein' a Morrie 8 he had bought from his star and herald money for twenty-five quid, but the V8 was Larry's pride and joy, and the day he drove it out of the car yard was the day that changed his life. He had gained the independence that he wanted.

CHAPTER TWO

Whatapu

Larry had met up with a French Fijian bloke whom he got on well with and the two of them were hardly apart. They both liked fishin' and that's basically what they did most of the time. If it wasn't Piha, it was Anawhata or the Nine Pin at the trecaherous entrance to the Manukau Harbour, the Manukau Bar bein' one of the most dangerous in the country. A whole shipload of sailors perished there one dark and stormy night on the naval vessel *Orpheus* with a plaque placed on the rocks in memoriam.

Denny and Larry spent night after night, sleeping in a cave on the Nine Pin rocks. They both had their surfcasters, Denny's bein' a hollow fibreglass state-of-the-art rod with a pfleuger running reel. Denny was a real master with this rig and could cast his line a bloody long way out. Larry settled for a home-made cane rod, which he had spent hours and hours, puttin' on the reel holder and eyes.

He had a Mitchell spinning reel, and that had to be the best.

Larry did a good job of casting this one out, but couldn't quite get as far as Denny.

One weekend the two of 'em decided to head out there for the weekend.

This was goin' to be a good weekend according to the moon and tides. Denny arrived at Larry's after work on the Friday night. All the gear was loaded up, ready for the big weekend and off the two of them went.

It was a good hour-and-a-half drive along a narrow, dusty road to their destination, but before that, they had to tackle the rigours of city driving, pickin' up a few supplies along the way, mainly food and ciggies.

Larry and Denny didn't drink a lot of booze, only the odd bottles Tom gave to them as they were too young to purchase any, bein' under twenty-one, but fags were different, Pall Mall plain bein' the favourite, which they promptly fired up as they headed out of the city, windin' their way around the country roads towards the west coast, Whatapu, and the Nine Pin rock.

It was close to 9 p.m. when they finally arrived, unloaded, and headed off in the direction of the beach. It was a good thirty-minute walk over the sandhills to the rocky outcrop of the Nine Pin. They had to time it right with the tide; if it were in, they would not have been able to get to the rocks, so the only time was from low tide till about a third incoming.

It was pitch-black that particular night, but the ol' Tilley lantern did the job of showing them the way. Trudging through the sand in the middle of the night was tough goin', Larry thinking to himself how hard it must have been for the blokes during the war as a lot of the guys were the same sixteen-year-old men as they were, the two of them carrying probably the same weighted packs as they did.

They arrived to the sound of the surf breaking on the beach not far from the Nine Pin. The only time there was surf there was when there was a big sea running, as these rocks were tucked inside the harbour bar.

Denny started yahooin' when he saw that the tide was out just enough for them to get to the rocks. They scrambled up on to a flat spot and made their way to a small cave they were to kip down for the night.

Larry was full of adrenalin and couldn't wait to get his line in the water, the best spot to cast bein' towards the harbour bar. They both baited up, Larry bein' the first in the water and was just headin' back to put his rod in a crack for support, and to light up a fag, when bang, there was a humongous strike on his line, Denny yellin' at the same time full of excitement. His rod bent to the max, Larry gave a good pull on his rod and was on! Denny was yellin' and shoutin' for the fact that he had just hooked up, and the two of them landed the first fish of the weekend, a couple of nice eight pounders. They fished on into the early hours of the morning until they had about a dozen fish flappin' about on the rocks, tied them on to a line, and hung them over into the sea to keep them fresh.

Larry suggested they grab a bit of kip before the sun came up, the best time for the biggies.

About five o'clock, Larry was woken up by a whisper from Denny that it was time for the onslaught. There was just about enough light to see but still had to use the Tilley lamp to make sure they were baitin' up properly. Denny was in first with Larry, casting out a couple of minutes, later, then both settling down for a fag and a cold pie they had bought on the way.

Things were rather quiet compared with earlier, but that's fishin' according to the rules so to speak, Larry and Denny just talking idle chatter.

Larry had just finished his fag and stood up to admire the daylight just starting to light up the surroundings, Denny wandering over against the rock face for a piss, when all the two of them could hear was the wizzing noise of Denny's Pfleuger as a fish took his line and started headin' out to sea. He grabbed for his bent over rod, struck, and started to play the good-sized fish, whatever it was. After a five-minute struggle he landed a good twelve pounder.

'You bloody beauty'! Larry gasped as Denny hauled the snapper on to the rocks.

Larry picked up his own rod at this stage and just as well because, bang, he was on! He could tell by the feel of it that it was a good fish, and it was another twelve pounder.

Larry and Denny had added about another eight to their catch, hangin' them in the water with the fish they had caught earlier, the two of them stopping for another well-deserved fag.

The sun was not quite up yet, but it was daylight, the surge of the sea racing up the rock face and back to where it came from, Larry and Denny taking in the sheer beauty of it all. What a fantastic place this was! So wild, so menacing, the sea, a crystal blue, the thunder of the surf on the ocean beach, all the sea birds goin' about their way, looking for any trace of food they could scavenge or hunt! Every now and again a mollymawk would let out a yodel as it swooped down towards the sea, turning and touching the water with its wing tip 'How bloody lucky are we?', they both thought.

Larry reached down for another fag, looked up to light it, his line of sight focusing on the catch they had in the water, and to his dismay, there was a monster shark havin' a feast of the day. Larry screamed at Denny the pair of 'em jumpin' to their feet, racing over towards the fish. What a friggin' monster! This shark was all of ten feet, a bloody big bronzy. Larry grabbed the line and hauled them further up the rocks so the surge of the waves would keep them wet, while Denny dealt with the bronzy with the gaff.

Jesus Christ! That was a close call, and the bastard had got to at least six of them and ruined about three.

Larry and Denny were pissed off, but it added a bit of excitement to the morning.

The lines were back in the water; Larry and Denny thinking that that was it, as once a shark turns up it's usually curtains for fishing, but not in this case. No sooner the lines hit the water, the fish were in the bag. These ones were monsters, twenty pounders plus. They were losin' gear left, right, and centre, but were riggin' up just as quick and back in the water. This barrage o' fish never stopped for a good three quarters of an hour until the boys had had enough and lounged back on the rock for another well-deserved fag, gloating over the twenty or more giant snapper they had caught, the sea surging over them, keeping them fresh.

Larry decided it was time to cook up a feed and proceeded to hunt around for any bits of driftwood that maybe lyin' about. There was not a bloody piece anywhere handy, so decided to browse about the other side of the rocks, sure enough, there was heaps.

He gathered up a handful, scrambling down into crevices where the sea had lodged ample pieces and headed back to the campsite. He was just roundin' a big boulder when Denny hollered out for him to get his arse over there pronto. Larry tore over to where Denny was gazing down into the water. Christ, all bloody mighty, there they were, two of the biggest flamin' sharks you'd have ever seen havin' a go at the snapper they had. The flamin' things were surfin' up on the swell, grabbin a mouthful o' snapper and wrigglin' back, their torsos clean outta the water. No matter what the boys did, it didn't deter these monsters, whackin' them with the gaff, rods, throwin' rocks, yellin', but to no avail. The boys stood there and just watched as the sharks near cleaned up their catch. 'Bastards,' yelled Larry and sat down on a rock damn near in tears.

Denny was also in the same predicament and sat down beside him, pullin' out the fags and offering one to Larry. The two o' 'em took down a few deep drags, turned and looked at each other and burst into laughter. 'Holy bloody shit', they couldn't believe it, a whole flamin' morning down the tubes, but that didn't perturb them, and after they had cooked up a feed of what was left, about three worth eating, they were both back into it.

The morning ticked by with the two boys hookin' up a few more good 'uns, the sun beatin' down on their vulnerable heads and scorchin' their exposed torsos. Come mid-afternoon, they decided to pack it in and head off back to the big smoke.

The trip home was full o' laughter and reminiscing about their night on the Nine Pin rocks and, of course, plenty of talk about the next big adventure.

They decided the next trip would be to Anawhata, and to accompany them, they both decided that ol' Tom deserved a trip away for the night.

It was all arranged with ol' Tom rearin' to go, the preceding week draggin' by at a real snail's pace.

Come Friday arvo, Larry had worked it out with Denny that he would pick him up after work, then head back, and pick up ol' Tom. Well, you wouldn't read about it; by the time Larry had picked up Denny and headed back for Tom, it was gettin' close to seven o'clock, and guess what, Tom had got home early, thinkin' they'd get away earlier and had got on the piss. He was bloody near three quarters gone.

Larry and Denny couldn't believe it, but not exactly surprised, knowin' full well that Tom loved his grog.

The boys bungled Tom into the ol' V8 and headed out towards the coast, this time bein' well prepared.

Anawhata was situated just a little further north up the coast from the Nine Pin, about ten miles and the next beach north of Piha. To get to the beach meant a hike down through the bush for a good thirty minutes, by way of a Department of Conservation track, which they had cut and maintained for public use. This was the norm throughout the Waitakere ranges, a small mountain range which ran from Titirangi to the south, through to where it petered out to the north at Bethells beach. The track flowed out on to a small horseshoe-shaped beach, upon which the surf pounded relentlessly, but this was not where the boys intended to go; they were makin' their way to a point that jutted out into the ocean. To get to this secret spot, so they thought, was just before the DOC track.

It was a track which led to a university study hut perched on a ridge leading out to the point. It was a good twenty minutes hike to the hut and then another twenty minutes down to the point. The track from the hut to the point was rather steep, like about forty degrees for the first fifteen minutes and then dropped damn near vertical on to the point.

Larry was concerned for Tom bein' pissed and all, so suggested to Denny that they camp down in the uni hut till ol' Tom sobered up a bit, which, of course, Denny agreed.

They headed off in the dark, Larry in front with the Tilley lamp, Tom in the middle, and Denny bringin' up the rear holdin' a big Jim torch.

This part of the hike was relatively easy goin' with Tom doin' the odd nosedive as they pushed their way through the heavy growth of flaxes that festooned the area. By the time they hit the uni hut, Tom was absolutely stuffed, pantin' and wheezin', floppin' himself down into a chair at the roughly built so-called table, which was the only bit of furniture in the place except for an over—and under bunk, which had been knocked up with a few pieces of rough sawn timber and straw type mattresses thrown on top.

Denny was the first to crash on them, whilst Larry cranked up the fire and set to knock up a nice hot cuppa. Tom, by this time, had chirped up a bit and was goin' on about what a breeze the trip to the hut was, completely unaware of what lay ahead. Larry and Denny threw each other a quick smirky grin, assuring Tom that he 'did well'.

Tom wasn't all that young, yet not that old at fifty and generally held good health, was always fairly fit, but a night on the turfs really kicked his arse in, and both the boys knew the next phase was goin' to pay its toll, especially with the fact that Tom didn't know that after the cuppa, a bite to eat, and about an hour's kip, they were venturing down into the toughest part of the expedition.

Larry was first to rise dead keen to get to the point before the dawn, and after giving Denny and Tom a shake up, they gathered up the gear and headed off, with Tom full of energy and by now had slept off a bit of the booze.

The track wasn't as bad as anticipated with the scrub becomin' a lot thinner the closer they got to the point, and by this time, Tom was whistling the ol' war song 'Colonel Bogie' with the tune gettin' louder and louder with each step, in fact, it was so invigorating that the boys joined in, and they whistled their way right on to the point.

They had timed it right; the daylight just starting to push its way to god zone, the boys hurrying to see who was first in the water.

Tom just took his time, casually unwinding his hand line ready for the big swing.

Denny had brought along an old onion sack, which he stuffed with some rotten old bait the boys had left over from the Nine Pin, tied a rope to it, and then tossed it into the water just beyond the rocks. Ol' Tom stood there scratchin' his thinning hair, asking Denny what that was all about, and Denny explaining about the abundance of crays in the area and that the sack was to catch them with.

'You see, the crays crawl on to the sack after the food, the claws get stuck, momentarily, in the twine, wait for a while, pull it in quickly and, walla, crayfish for bait!' Tom couldn't comprehend the boys using crays for bait, but as the day progressed, he realised the place was lousy with 'em.

The first cast was fresh mullet bait, all puttin' on big chunks. Tom's theory was 'Big bait, big fish' and how true could it be with the three of them baggin' monster snapper all mornin', with Tom havin' a whale of a time even though he was hung over to the max.

Come midday, they had all had enough, so decided to call it a day.

Denny and Larry packed up the gear, whilst Tom head, tailed, and gutted the snapper to make the load lighter for the gruelling hike back up the cliff face and towards the hut.

Denny took the lead this time as Larry wanted to be behind Tom to give him a heave ho, if need be, and that's just what he did need.

Tom, even though he was sober by now, was not at all well from the booze, and the trip to the hut really put paid to any visions of joy.

He was absolutely well and truly fucked. Larry and Denny, even though they were youngsters, paid the price, with them all crashing into the hut for a well-deserved cuppa. Tom makin' his way to the bunks,

Denny and Larry gathered around the table for an analysis of their morning's ordeal, tryin' to get a word in over Tom's absolutely, deafening snoring. Hell's teeth, it was wicked.

After they had all had a feed, a cuppa, and a kip, they gathered up the packs and headed off back to the big smoke.

The following day, Larry and Denny got together around at Larry and Tom's flat, havin' a few beers and a bit of a barbe, Tom had done a great job of preparing the fish, so it was fish and snacks for lunch.

Bobby had turned up with a couple of her mates, which kept Denny happy as he was a bit smitten on Bobby, and Larry was left to the pick o' the rest of them. He had his eye on one sheila whom he half-pie knew as Bobby had bought her around a few times, but that's as far as the boys could go as Viv was to call around to pick them up, what, with Bobby bein' a baby and all, Viv had to keep an eye on her, but good ol' Bobby stuck to her ways and, after only bein' with Viv a few months, was soon knockin' on Tom's door for a bed.

Bobby stayed with Tom, goin' to the local school for a few months until she was arseholed out and before ya knew it, she was doin' dishes in a girls' home. She was a toughie, all right.

Larry and Denny just cruised about for a few more months, shootin' into town in the coupé, gettin' into a few scraps, pickin' up sheilas, goin' fishin'; life was becomin' humdrum.

One night, the two lads were down the waterfront in Auckland city doin' a bit o' night fishin' when outta the blue Denny piped up and suggested they both buggered off up north for an adventure.

Neither of them by this time had much money left, so they drove down to drivers' servo in Mt Roskill. They both knew the owner there as it was their local fill-up joint and casually asked if they could have a tank o' gas if they left some sort of security. Sure enough, they drove out with a full tank o' gas, minus a wrist watch and a spare tyre. It was fantastic: a beautiful night and an adventure ahead, but first, they had to pick up a few clothes from home. They went to Denny's, grabbed what he needed, and then off round to Larry's. By this time, it was gettin' close to midnight, but that didn't deter either of them as they were on a mission.

The lads arrived at Larry's, piled out of the coupé, and bounded inside, full of excitement only to have the whole scenario flattened at the sight of ol' Tom, pissed as a fart, crashed out in front of the kerosene heater.

Unbeknown to Tom, because of his drunken state, his leg was so close to the element that it had burnt the skin off his foreleg, and, bein' basically unconscious, had not even woken up. The two boys looked at each other with great despair, what the hell next! They quickly roused Tom, who wasn't bein' that co-operative and set about to try and attend to the wound. It was a hellava mess; the skin had broken and the flesh had started to cook. How on earth it hadn't woken him up was, to the boys utter dismay, a surprise!

Denny grabbed a basin of cold water, while Larry hunted about for some bandages, and the two of them doused his leg. Ol' Tom kicked up a great fuss, tellin' the pair o' them to piss off and leave him alone. He said that he had had worse than that, seen ten times worse than that during the war, and that it was only a scratch.

Larry and Denny felt bad about it as they drove off into the night, headin' for the far north. Out came the fags and on went the radio, and the both of them relieved they were on their way, headin' outta the big smoke.

CHAPTER THREE

The Far North

They cruised on for a good hour or so, stoppin' for a piss on the side of the road from time to time and just generally havin' a good ol' laugh; they were both happy and carefree on their way to who knows where. It was just breakin' daylight as they drove into Wellsford, a small country town known for its dairy farms and cattle.

Denny suggested they stop and see if they could grab a bite to eat, but bein' so early, nothin' was open yet, apart from a bakery, which was in full swing, goin' hard, baking the local bread. Larry beckoned Denny to stop and ask if they could grab a loaf of hot bread, to which the owner obliged. The boys got talkin' to the owner and explained they were on an adventure mission and were lookin' for any work wherever they could find it. Much to their amazement, the bakery owner knew of a farmer, just outta town, who was lookin' for a couple o' farm hands, so it was into the coupé, and off the two of them went in search of their first real adventure.

After driving for a good twenty minutes, they finally found the farm. It was a fairly barren lookin' place, with an old homestead sittin' in the middle o' a paddock with a few trees scattered about the front lawn. The two lads pulled up at the front gate and hopped out of the coupé. They weren't exactly the farming lookin' type of blokes, v8 coupé, dressed mainly in black, Denny, with the look of an Apachie Indian, straight black shoulder-length hair, covered in tattoos, but a big beaming smile, exposing a row of white pearly teeth and standing nearly six foot. On the other hand, Larry was of solid build, around five foot nine, broad in the shoulders, tapering to the waist in a muscular stance, his hair dropping to his shoulders in glistening wavy locks. The pair of them lookin' like a couple o' gangsters if you didn't know them at all and what they really were.

The farmer greeted them at the back door, asking of their business, eyes moving the two of 'em, up and down. After a few words and confidence building, they were both welcomed inside to talk business. Upon entering the kitchen, there, sittin' at the table, havin' breakfast, were five of the most beautiful girls the boys had seen ever, they thought, ranging from about thirteen to twenty. Larry quickly glanced at Denny, and they both understood what the other was thinking.

The farmer introduced them to his daughters very wryly and offered them a seat. Larry and Denny just didn't know where to look as these girls were so stunningly beautiful; however, after a lot of laughter and gettin' to know each other, they were offered the job under one condition: they were to keep well outta the way from his daughters. Well, the boys agreed, of course. Just to see them was enough for them to be satisfied.

They were shown to their digs which was a two-roomed sleepout at the rear of the house, only a few steps, in fact, from the back door. Larry and Denny grabbed their gear from the coupé and settled in for the day as they had started work immediately, much to there disgust, they were hoping to have a bit of a look about the place, but this farmer was a hard ol' bastard and called a spade a spade. A tall sinewy bloke with sun-dried skin, his face lookin' like a dried up caraway seed planted on his pin head, attached to narrow sloping shoulders. He strode about like a baby giraffe taking about six-foot strides with every step. His wife's a proper busybody. Short, fat, huge tits but a lovely woman, kind, and gentle.

The boys were shown around the milking shed, Larry taking it all in as he had had a little bit to do with milkin' cows on his grandfather's mate's farm down the Waikato. It was a six doubled-up walk-through shed, with the lean-to barely high enough for Denny to get under, let alone the owner. After a bit of question asking and information gathering,

Denny had to break the ice and ask the farmer his name again. To their embarrassment, 'What, you've forgotten already?' he bleated but finally blurted out, 'Dick, can't you remember? And this is Doris,' pointing to his wife. Thank God, that's sorted, the boys thought.

The rest of the day was fluffin' about, doin' odd jobs in the hay barn, workshop, fixin' bits and pieces, and just gettin' the feel. Before they knew it, the cows were bein' brought in for milking. It was Doris and the two eldest girls' job; 280 cows was a big herd back in the sixties and after a good four hours, it was all over. Larry and Denny hadn't a clue what they had in store for them on that farm. It was four hours of hell, with Doris and Dick yellin' and carryin' on like a couple of lunatics; the only good thing about it was the girls. They had turned out in force to watch the two boys workin', gigglin' and flirtin' the whole time under the watchful eye of Dick.

That evening was rather pleasant for Larry and Denny as the girls gave them all the attention they needed till Dick ordered them all to bed and told the boys to get some sleep; it was four o'clock start in the mornin'. The boys could hardly drag themselves outta bed that mornin', but once they had had a cuppa, they were fit and ready to get into it—same ol' scenario that morning as it was the previous day, yellin' and shoutin' at the cows, shit everywhere, but gettin' back to the house for breaky was a bonus 'cause the girls were there.

The day went by without a hitch with the two of them busy cleaning out the overflow from the farm dam and general farm duties, fencing, digging the odd hole, and grubbin' ragwort. There was one bonus, and that was that Doris could bloody well cook lunch and was like a banquet with all the roast goodies, lamb, spuds, kumara, everything and to top it all off, five lovely girls to talk to even though Dick didn't like it.

A couple of more days had ticked by and soon the boys had been there for five days. Their rapport with two of the girls in particular was becoming more than talkin' and the girls gettin' hotted up. Dick had noticed this and was starting to keep them from being around Larry and Denny by giving them chores to do in the evenings. The two eldest girls had local farmer's sons who where smitten on them, but the two middle girls where makin' a beeline for the boys, not that Larry and Denny minded, in fact, they tried their utmost to put on a good show. It was around one in the morning on the sixth night when Denny nudged

Larry. There was someone outside the sleepout snoopin' about. The boys sneaked to the door and slowly edged it open, no one there. They ventured outside with Larry leadin' the way when all of a sudden he felt a hand on his shoulder. He swung around quickly and was about to clout whoever was there, but, to his surprise, all he saw was this beautiful woman, standing in front of him. 'Holy fuck,' he whispered. 'What are you doin' here?' Denny poked his head out just to be smothered by the other sister.

They had sneaked out of the house to be with the boys who wasted no time in takin' them into the cabin. They couldn't believe it and soon were stark naked and screwin' their little arses off. After it was all over, the girls quickly snuck back to the house, but it was not all good. Dick had smelt a rat and was just comin' into the kitchen when the girls walked in. Well, if you'd ever heard a bomb go off! He was like a rampant bull. 'I'm gonna kill those little arseholes,' he yelled. Larry and Denny hadn't even had time to get back to bed and were grinnin' from ear to ear, havin' a smoke and a chat. They heard the ruckus and thought their day had come.

Doris had also risen gettin' her spoke in. After ten minutes or so, there was a knock on the door, guess who? Dick didn't have much to say as Denny stood in the doorway not lettin' him in and with Larry as backup, he didn't have a shit show.

The boys laughed their heads off as they drove up the country road, a pocket full o' money, as Dick had paid them out. Whew, what a start to their adventure and what a good one! Chalk that one up!

It was too early for the pub to be open so the boys drifted into a cafe and sat down to a great breaky of bacon and eggs. They hung about the town till after twelve waitin' for the pub to open, grabbed a dozen crate o' Lion Red and headed north.

Larry was the allocated driver that sunny arvo cruisin' along at around 40 mph just takin' it all in. Denny cracked open a long neck and handed it to Larry at the same instance crackin' one for himself. They both took a long swig of the cool nectar thinkin' how great things were for them both and the thought of the night before fresh in their loins.

By the time the lads got to the foot o' the Brynderwyns, a small mountain range dividing the far north from the rest o' New Zealand, they where feeling the effects o' the Lion red. Larry was gettin' pissed and Denny was well on the way, both o' em stuffed from all the laughin' they had been doin'. They decided to have a bit o' a rest, so Larry pulled the coupé into a siding. They polished off the remaining beers and crashed out.

It was around 1 a.m. when they finally came to. Larry risin' first, his whole body achin' from the awkward way he had been sleepin', crunched up in the front seat. Denny had a few more brains and was still snorin' his head off in the dicky seat at the back.

After sittin' there, gazin' into space, Larry decided to make a move. He still felt a little bit pissed and when he opened the door to step outside for a leak, his body didn't respond and tumbled out on to the gravel.

'Fuck, fuck, fuck,' he mumbled. The commotion woke Denny, and he was just as worse for wear, his body achin' from head to toe. It was as black as the inside of a coal mine, and to make it even worse, the fog had come in, and they were lucky to see five feet in front o' 'em.

Larry kicked the ol' V8 into life, fired up a fag, and slowly headed into the night. Denny was still curled up in the backseat, but not for long as Larry was naggin' him to wake up. It was so black with the fog and all, Larry suggested Denny to walk in front o' the coupé to guide the way. It took all of two hours for them to reach the summit.

Larry gave Denny a break from humpin' it and took over downhill. Denny wasn't happy at all that he had walked uphill, but as Larry explained, he 'wasn't to know where the summit was!'. Denny assured him he would get back somehow laughin' as he said it. Soon they were nearly half way down, and the daylight was pushin' its way through the fog. It was just enough to be able to see where they were goin', so Denny beckoned Larry aboard, and off they went slowly makin' their way down on to the Waipu plains.

The fog had lifted about eight feet, enough to allow them to see the road ahead. It was like they were drivin' through a road to nowhere, an eerie feelin', the two lads hardly sayin' a word, puffin' on ciggies and feelin' really, really like shit! All they could hear in the deathly quiet surroundings was the dull throb o' the V8 and the odd fart they were both lettin' loose from time to time. Finally Denny broke the silence and pulled over stating he wanted to take a piss. Larry was happy with this as he was bustin' also.

It was nearin' 8 a.m. when they chugged their way into Whangarei, the main centre for the far north. There wasn't a sole to be seen nor a shop open anywhere. The boys were starvin' and desperately hunted about for some signs of life, and bein' a Sunday was bloody hard to find in Whangarei in the sixties.

Denny headed the coupé up the main street and on to the main drag north when, to their surprise, there was a gas station, and it was open. They filled the coupé with gas, grabbed half a dozen cold pies, and headed off.

Kawakawa was a quaint little town nestled in a valley at the upper reaches of the Kawakawa river. It was one of the hub towns of the Bay of Islands, a resort area where everyone in New Zealand loved to go for their vacation. Denny knew of some people there that might give them a job and after askin' about the town they finally had an address.

The farm was outta town and towards the Bay itself. The road was dirt and winding, but finally, they made it turning on to a private road down to the homestead.

A young lad about nineteen greeted them as they drove up to the implement shed. He introduced himself as Joe, a well-built, blond-headed, clean-shaven cow cocky's son, crew cut hairstyle, check shirt, jeans and work boots, fit as a buck rat and twice as dangerous. The lads explained what they were after and were soon munchin' on home-made scones and sipping on a hot cuppa. It was introductions all round: brothers, sisters, Mum, and Dad, all hard-workin' and proud family, the girls bein' a'la natural, hair up in a bun, long skirts, and buckled up shoes. One o' the bros and the ol' man were even wearing braces to hold up their trousers.

The lads later discovered they belonged to the Commonwealth Covenant Church, a bit like Amish people, but this was a welcomed break for the lads as they made them feel like one o' the family as soon as they arrived, inviting them, despite their appearance, to stay as long as they liked until they found permanent work. They didn't need any extra hands.

Larry and Denny had a ball living with these people, horse ridin', rabbit huntin', workin' in the bush, haulin' logs although they weren't paid. Larry and Denny felt they were helpin' also it was a way of showin' their appreciation for what they were doin' for them both.

One evening, all the men decided to go for a moonlight ride on the horses. The farm bordered the road on one boundary, ran away from there with grazing paddocks, then plunging down into thick native New Zealand bush, and a river on the other. This is where they were headed.

Five horses and eight dogs headed off down the farm track into the bush.

Joe always talked of spirits and Maori burial grounds down by the river and even informed the lads of a grave site of a Maori princess.

Once a year, the local Maori tribe gathered there to pay their respects. Joe also talked of the spirits frequenting the cowshed from time to time. 'Yea, right', thought Larry, havin' a sideways glance at Denny with a grin.

It was one o' the best nights the lads had been on: the fresh air, the smell o' the horse sweat, the dogs boundin' about in excitement, racin' ahead o' the horses and back again yappin' and barkin', everyone jokin' and laughin'; it was paradise.

The pack was approachin' the area where the princess's grave was. It was a rather steep decline and the horses were diggin' in to get a hold.

The dogs were about twenty metres in front o' the horses, when, a few o' 'em stopped dead in their tracks, focusing on the bush and the track ahead. All of a sudden, the bloody horses were rearin' up and whinin' and snortin'. The dogs had all opened up barkin' now and a few o' 'em hightailed it back up the track as fast as they could go. No matter what anyone did, they just couldn't get the horses to venture any further down the track towards the grave o' the princess. After a good five minutes, the men couldn't hold the horses any longer, dropped the reins, and the horses bounded back up the track on to the grass paddock, followed by the remainin' dogs. Everyone climbed down off the horses, not uttering a bloody word, the dogs panting, the horses frothin' at the bit, and all freakin' out.

'What the hell happened there?' Denny was the first to talk.

Joe stood there like a stone statue in the moonlight; nobody knew what to say. Larry still had the hair on his back and arms standin' up, and he had a really weird feelin'. Joe was in shock as he thought all the stories he told them were just myth, and he was only tryin' to scare them, but everyone now realised it was no myth.

The weird feelin' remained with Larry for days after that night.

Kawakawa had a good nightclub, the Casablanca. Larry and Denny decided to go for a look one Saturday night.

Joe asked if he could tag along, which was no problem to Denny and Larry. It turned out that Joe was a frequent visitor to the club and also had a reputation as a scrapper. Larry noticed he was dressed similar to his work clobber, but he had a new pair o' boots which he called his 'fightin' boots'. Larry thought it a good idea not to get on the wrong side o' Joe!

The club was really pumpin' with the local Maori boys twangin' away on stage and all the spunky chicks you could find in Kawakawa.

Larry and Denny were hangin' for a beer but were disappointed to find that the place was dry. Only bloody Coke! Oh, well, that would have to do besides there were plenty o' sheilas there to keep 'em busy.

The two o' 'em were havin' a ball and had lined up a couple o' girls they were sure were goin' to turn it up havin' a dance or two and a snog here an there had the girls fizzin' at the bung. The night went on with Larry and Denny positive by this time all was on. Joe had been outside the club most o' the evening lookin' for a scrap. He had a reputation there and not many blokes wanted to take him on. Suddenly there was a commotion in the foyer.

The club was situated down a flight of stairs, with the ticket box bein' at the bottom and a door accessing the club. Denny was first out. He was no slug when it came to a stoush. Larry got there in time to see Denny bendin' down to pick Joe up off the floor.

An old Maori bloke had been at the ticket box pissed and tryin' to get into the club. Joe was only trying to help his mate sellin' the tickets to get rid o' him when the ol' bugger king hit him and down he went. Well, it was all on; when Joe got up he smacked this bloke that hard he flew through the door and into the club. This bloke was in his midthirties to the seventeen-year-olds that frequented the club, but unfortunately, a lot of his Whanau or family, were there, and they streamed out into the foyer to have a go! Joe had already got to the top o' the stairs tellin' the lads later he had a better chance in the open, but there was only one problem. Larry and Denny were left to pick up the pieces. They stood shoulder to shoulder in the stair way slammin' anyone who got too close, the thing was some o' his family were big buggers and proved a fair match for them.

Denny and Larry inched their way to the top o' the stairs leavin' behind a pile o' people at the bottom. They managed to reach the street where Joe was waitin' in a boxers' stance, ready to flatten anyone who came up.

Some o' 'em managed to get by, and it was all on in the street; by this time it was anyone's and everyone's until the local cop turned up. It was over. How one cop could stop all that had the boys baffled, but the locals respected the cop there and respect they did.

Larry and Denny nursed their bruises for days after that night and wondered how it may have turned out if Joe hadn't of been such a bloody redneck, he didn't have a scratch on him.

Time moved on and things were changin' between Larry and Denny. Larry had scored a job on a chicken farm and was feelin' quite at home with a couple o' bob in his pocket. Denny had a job on a dairy farm down the road, but wasn't happy and tried to get Larry to move on. He had seen a job advertised down the King Country on a sheep station.

They wanted two general hands, but Larry was happy doin' what he was and eventually Denny packed up and left.

Both the lads were headin' for their twenties. Larry comin' up eighteen. He felt he had to find something secure for ol' Tom as he had got himself into a mess in Auckland, so Larry had arranged for him to live on the chook farm with him; besides, his boss had a daughter, beautiful body, but not really an oil paintin', but that didn't worry Larry. He was gettin' it off every night and sometimes durin' the day when he took her huntin'.

The months ticked by with Larry goin' about his work amongst the chooks. He had the job of delivering eggs to stores and supermarkets in Whangarei, so once a week he had a break away from the boss's daughter.

A bloke, up the road, had a dairy farm and was lookin' for a farm hand to help with the milkin'. Larry jumped at the chance; although there were no women there, he had noticed pieces of an ol' motorbike in the garage.

It was a Royal Enfield 250 single banger. He told Larry if he could put it back together, he could have it. This was an opportunity of a lifetime for Larry. He had sold the ol' coupé and was hangin' out for a motorbike.

It didn't take him long to get it up and runnin' and was soon doin' trips back and forth to Whangarei. He later got rid of the Royal Enfield and upgraded to a 350 bathy Triumph, a bike he had always wanted, but only the ccs weren't up to it. He would have liked a 650 but was happy with the one he had until his neighbour rode it, pissed and bent it up, fucked it completely.

Ol' Tom had scored a job as maintenance painter at the hospital. He had a small cabin as a home but was quite happy pottering about there. He had knocked back on his drinking, but only during the week because the hospital authorities had given him a warning about the booze.

Not only that, he was tryin' to crack on to some o' the married nurses there, not that there was a shortage, but he was gettin' pissed and not realising what he was doin'. He managed to meet a single woman, who soon quietened him down. The first bonk he had had since Viv, and that would have been a good five years.

Larry had a girlfriend in Kawakawa. She was the winner of the local beauty queen competition, a real stunner, so he spent a lot of his time at her house when her parents were away on business.

Audry was his first real girl friend and a discovery lesson of bein' in love.

Audry was the typical country beauty: blonde hair, beautiful body, rounded breasts, and lovely little bum. Her face was outta the movies. Her golden locks framing beautiful blue eyes, dark eyelashes, small straight nose, full red lips, and a smile a bloke would melt over.

Not only that, she had a lovely nature and was a very caring woman. Even at seventeen and livin' in the country, she still had an old head on her shoulders and kept Larry on his toes in the manners department.

Larry could cope with this, though, because when he was naked next to her, nothing else in the world mattered to him.

Every time his lips met hers, he enjoyed the soft sweet taste and the smell of her breath and the look in her eyes. The feel of her perfect breasts sent Larry awal as he caressed her, down over the smooth skin of her flat tummy to her silky mound. When they made love, it was as if life had momentarily halted, and they were in a time warp to nowhere, as all they felt was love!

The relationship with Audry became very intense with time. It was draining Larry's energy, just tryin' to keep other blokes away from her.

Although they loved each other very much, peer pressure finally drew them apart.

Audry went on to win again the following year eventually movin' to Whangarei. Her father had been transferred as executive of the dairy company so she had to leave. This devastated Larry for a time, but because he had been the boyfriend of the beauty queen meant that all the girls in town wanted a piece o' him, and he was kept very busy bein' of service to all the babes in the area, not that Larry minded.

Apart from the girls, goin' fishin' and farm work things weren't good for Larry; it was time to move on. Ol' Tom seemed OK with what he was doin' and gave Larry his blessing, and he moved back to Auckland.

He had no transport, and he'd been relyin' on the use of Tom's Austin Cambridge. The trip on the train to Auckland was a slow uncomfortable journey. Viv was there to meet him at New Lynn station and took him home to a feed of roast beef and spuds.

CHAPTER FOUR

A New Beginning

Rupert owned a house in Auckland's west. His ex-wife had been living there but had buggered off with a couple o' Indians, so the house was handed back to him. Viv had spent her money doin' up the place, new paths, landscaped the garden with new paint and paper. Rupert had been laid off from his job, so they had decided to sell the house and buy a business. They managed to crack up a deal with a couple on the shore. Swap the house for a dairy. It was a big move for them as they were goin' into unknown waters.

Larry had scored a job, so the move meant he would have to travel to the west from the Bays. Viv came to the rescue by purchasing a utility truck for the business, but allowed Larry to call it his own as long as he kept up the maintenance on it, and they could use it to pick up stock from the warehouse.

Larry was wrapped it was a fairly late model Vanguard ute.

Larry loved his job and worked his guts out every day hand-diggin' trenches and layin' pipes. His boss was a fantastic bloke and took a lot of interest in Larry, encouraging him to go to night school and get his qualifications upgraded. He had a brother as a labourer who was a little autistic but worked like a trooper.

The two of them did most of the work, whilst the boss went about organising things.

It wasn't long before Larry became a number-one tradesman and gained a reputation as one of the best in his field, having the highest recognition in the business.

The move to the bays was paying its toll on Larry travelling to the west, so he managed to get a job with one o' the local plumbers as the head drainlayer. This job was fantastic, and he even had the use of a Commer truck for work. The local council had outlayed millions to install a new sewer system in the East Coast Bays, so there was an abundance of work.

It wasn't long before Larry chummed up with some o' the local lads, most o' 'em bein' into surfin'. This was a far cry from the black jeans and leather jackets Larry had been used to, but there was something really refreshing in surfin', and it wasn't long before he was in full swing goin' to all the beaches in the north and south, chasing the elusive big wave.

Larry's newfound friends were a great bunch o' guys and to top it off, they had a big following of gorgeous women. Weekends were surf, surf, surf, women, women, women, booze, booze, booze, and party, party, party. His best mates were a bunch o' hard out seaweeds and surfin' was it.

Not only that, but they were into cars as well. Mark I and II Zephyrs were the go, but some of the guys had to be content with Austin A40s and the like.

Larry was in the top league with his vanguard. This was great for weekends away, throwing a mattress in the back, sleeping wherever for the night. One of the best known spots was Ahipara in the far north. It was a left-hand break, and if the surf was up, one could ride a wave for a good five minutes because the break followed the shoreline before crashin' on to the white sand of ninety-mile beach.

It was 6 a.m. in the morning. The lads had had a long trip from Auckland the day before. It was dark when they arrived, so couldn't quite estimate the size of the surf, but by the way it was crashing on to the beach, it was big.

Stewy was first, yellin' to the boys to get the fuck out here and take a look. They all stood there in awe. It was a good ten to fifteen feet and glassy surging along the point break in a fashion to donate the perfect wave.

Stewy was already runnin' down the beach, his bronzed body glistening in the early morning sunrise. He was a favourite with the women: tall, blond hair, and a good body and because he was a charm with the girls, he earned the nickname 'Casa'. It wasn't long before all the boys were makin' their way along the rocks to the end of the point to grab the longest ride, the surf thunderin' past like a convoy of locos.

Casa had already plunged into the surf, followed by Larry, Bones, Mikey, Al, and Chook.

The surf was huge, and once in the water, it seemed twice as big as it looked on land. Larry picked up a nice break and surfed until it petered out on the left, giving him an easy paddle back to where the waves were startin' to pick up. All the boys were catchin' good waves, some o' 'em up for a good minute or so. Larry looked behind him to see a monster formin' up about 100 metres out. He paddled like a possessed turtle until he could feel the surge pick him up and away he went. It was a good four-metre monster; Larry was yellin' for joy as he screamed down the face at what seemed a hundred miles an hour.

Larry bein' a goofy footer was really at home with this break, and as he hit the foot o' the wave, dropped in, and climbed back up to the peak. He was so invigorated, he forgot about the world and was one with this monster. Up and down, back and forth he went droppin' and climbin', which seemed an eternity. This wave didn't want to end. It was as if it was made for him, specifically, and didn't want him to leave. After a good two minutes, Larry could see the beach loomin' in the distance.

Every time, it seemed like it was going to end; the wave somehow picked up again and pushed Larry closer and closer to the beach. For some reason, Larry just couldn't cut out of this wave; it was as if he was part of it, and as the beach got closer, he realised it was too late.

The wave picked up on the peak to at least five metres. Larry screamed down the wave with a wall of whitewater behind him so big he knew he was in deep shit. It slammed him right to the bottom of the ocean floor: sand, shells, seaweed was all he could see. The swirling and the bubbles disorientated him to a degree he didn't know where the fuck he was.

Over and over he went, his body twistin', turnin', and smashin' on to the sand, gaspin' for breath. He thought it was all over. His mind was startin' to go blank. He could see little black specks in his vision, all but the poppin' sound in his ears.

Larry opened his eyes, and he could feel something warm on his body. It was the sun. He struggled to his feet but didn't know where he was. The wave had so much force that it had driven him right up and on to the sandhills far up the beach; he knew right then he had caught a rouge.

Larry looked around for his new Wallace surfboard and noticed something pokin' outta the sand. It was part of it, the wave had smashed it to pieces, but Larry was unperturbed as that ride had to be the most exciting thing he had ever experienced apart from sex. That day would be with him forever.

Bones had seen it all as he was walking back from a ride he had just had and strode over to where Larry was, exclaiming how unbelievable the whole thing was.

That night around the campfire was chinwaggin' to the extreme. Not one of the lads really noticed the beautiful women that they had brought along. It wasn't until they were all talked out and a few beers under their belts that the girls got what they had been waitin' for:, attention!

One of the girls had an eye for Larry. Shelly was still goin' to school. She was tall for a girl and reached contact with Larry's eyes.

Her athletic body turned Larry on. With long curly blonde hair and blue eyes, she was a woman Larry had to have. Although she was only fifteen, it wouldn't be long before she turned sixteen. He dated Shelly for a good three months before he even had a look in; Shelly was a virgin.

By the time she had turned sixteen, their relationship was flourishing. They both enjoyed the same things, and Shelly bein' an easy-goin' type, never had a problem packin' up and pissin' off for the weekend. It was one night on the beach that Shelly finally consented giving herself to the man she had fallen in love with.

Larry and Shelly spent nearly every weekend away, fishin' and surfin'; their relationship had blossomed into a partnership of love and trust.

Their compatibility couldn't be better and before they knew it, she was pregnant! It was a time in their lives where they had to make a decision that could either make their lives better or ruin it forever.

Shelly had to break the news to her parents. It wasn't good. Shelly's ol' man was someone Larry didn't connect with at all: domineering, know-all, and sarcastic.

On the other hand, her mum was a sympathetic type and kept her cool. The ol' man threw a wobbly and had a panic attack.

'You'll have to get married. All my friends and business associates will look down on me.' A bloody social climber. Shelly's mom suggested she have an abortion, but her ol' man insisted they get married.

For a few weeks, Larry and Shelly tried all ways to lose the baby—drinking hot Coca cola, then plunging into a cold bath, and fucking as hard as they could, thinking the baby would fall out—anything at all to induce a miscarriage. Shelly's ol' man was still adamant they get married.

It was around smoko when Larry's boss called on to the job with the news that Shelly had had a miscarriage. Larry drove to her home where she was resting. She wrapped her arms around him so tight his face turned red.

They were married a few months later.

Life carried on for them both, with Shelly and Larry securing a quaint little house down by the beach. They socialised frequently and often had friends around for dinner parties. Larry had got himself involved in a dive club and gained the right to edit. Shelly, bein' a good typist, was also involved, and the two o' 'em spent evenings compilin' newsletters.

Larry had drifted away from the surf scene, thinking it was not really for him but enjoyed it nonetheless. By this time, Larry was working in his own business in the construction industry and was doin' rather well.

Shelly had her job as secretary, so between them money was free flowin'. Larry had a few good mates he went diving with, most o' 'em in the building game. Whenever there was a perfect day for diving, it was down tools and outta there.

Shelly came along on most of the dive weekends up and down the coast campin' out, mingling with the other chicks, waitin' for the boys to come back from a dive.

They had just finished dinner. Larry wandered over to the couch and sat down to watch a bit o' telly. Shelly sat beside him and put her arms around him. It seemed a bit odd to Larry. She was more affectionate than usual. He had also noticed she was looking really beautiful in the last few weeks. He understood everything after Shelly told him she was pregnant. Larry was ecstatic—a baby!

The news was good news, but Larry thought he would have liked to wait a couple more years before they had children, but nevertheless, it was fantastic.

Seven months later, after a good six hours of labour, Shelly gave birth to a beautiful little girl, Larry standin' beside her throughout the whole ordeal.

It was certainly a proud moment for them both, and they decided to call her Sarah.

It was Christmas and the club was away up north for a two-week jaunt around the Cavalli islands on the east coast of the far north.

Larry had bought a new tent for him, Shelly, and Sarah, along with a gas stove, chilly bin, and all the bits and pieces you would need on a campin' holiday. Sarah was nearly six months old, a good age to take away campin'. Larry and Shelly were both excited and loaded up the ol' Vanguard and headed off. It was a long drive to Matauri bay.

Two thirds of the journey had sealed roads but the other third had windin' dirt roads and bein' summer, dusty.

Everyone had the same idea and that was to head north.

The traffic was mind-blowin', bumper to bumper most of the way. It was late arvo when the ol' Vanguard rounded a bend and, there it was, Matauri Bay. What an absolutely awesome sight—the Cavalli Islands reaching out into the blue Pacific, Matauri bay with its sweeping beach, and dotted along the foreshore, dozens of tents! It seemed they weren't the first ones there.

Larry edged the ute around the winding dirt road and down on to the flats and Matauri bay. Most of the boys were there already and some o' 'em still pitchin' their tents. Larry found a spot amongst the array next to ol' Duncan. Duncan was an ex-biker, gone good but was still loyal to the cause. He was a few years elder than Larry, meanin' eight years, but a good mate to have. Duncan had dragged a couple of his biker mates along with him. They were blokes you don't want to upset, but loved their fishin' and divin' as much as the next bloke. These guys didn't get around in beach garb; it was all jeans and leather jackets, which put Larry back into his comfort zone.

Larry set about pitchin' the tent, Shelly lendin' a hand where she could, in between tendin' to Sarah, unpackin' the necessary utensils to cook up a feed. It wasn't long before all was done, and they both stretched back with an ice-cold Lion Red with the rest o' the pack. The following morning was like someone had dropped a silence bomb. It was dead still and eerie, the sea like a mill pond. Everyone was up and about early even though some were hung over.

Larry didn't own a boat, but there were more than enough boats there to satisfy all.

It was early morning when Larry first got his head wet. The whole crew had ventured out to one of the outer reefs of the Cavalli group. It consisted of an area approximately three acres with a couple of bommies protruding up out of the crystal-clear water.

The eastern side of the reef dropped off suddenly to a good forty metres.

Between the bommies was a deep gut of around ten metres, teaming with fish of all shapes and sizes. Larry made his way to this area first with speargun and float in tow. Bein' a 'spearfishin' club, this was paradise. Snapper, red snapper, blue moki, pink and blue maomao, porae, and best of all kingis.

The visibility was a good twenty metres. Larry loaded his gun and slowly patrolled the gut. He noticed a nice snapper hiding amongst the weed. He took a deep breath and silently slipped beneath the surface.

Snapper of this type are known to spearos as kelpies. They always hung about hidin' in the kelp, which abounds in New Zealand waters.

They are solitary individuals and very shy, so stealth is a must if one is huntin' them.

He slipped down behind a rock, just bein' able to get a glimpse of his foe. The fish hadn't seen him, and it was a beauty. Arm outstretched, gun in hand, he slid around the rock and let loose nailin' the snapper with a kill shot to the lateral line. This was the first of five on that day.

Some o' the boys were diving the 'drop off', so Larry made his way to where they were all floatin' on the surface, gazin' into the depths below.

Every now and then, one dived down, tryin' to draw the kingis to the surface to no avail. Three of the lads, including Larry all dived at once pluckin' the rubbers on their spearguns like a guitar sendin' out a song into the depths. This had done the trick. Larry gazed into the blue only to see some small dots venturin' up from the depths. They got bigger and bigger as they got closer, and when about four metres from them, they changed shape as these giant Kingis turned side on to have a look at the underwater musicians.

The boys nearly choked on their snorkels as these fish were a good eighty to ninety pounds. Duncan fired first, nailin' a good fish, and Larry was next. The rest of the school was wonderin' what the fuck was goin' on 'cos they all just kept millin' about the divers oblivious of the danger that was before them. It was made clear to the boys that these fish had never seen humans before.

The Cavallis, especially where they were diving, were virtually untouched by divers. In the sixties there were very few spearfishermen and to get to a spot like they were in was a spearo's dream. All the boys nailed good size kingis, the biggest bein' a good ninety-five pounds. That evenin' saw the boys preparing the fish for smokin'.

There were around 100 people gathered in the bay, so each and every family had a feed o' fish and the smoked kingis.

Each day was a good one, with the weather bein' as still as a cemetery. The first week went by without a hitch. Everybody was gettin' on well.

It was the second night of the second week when things started to get outta hand. All the divin' had started to wear off for the ones that weren't devoted spearos. Because o' this out come, the piss and every day was a piss up. Arguments started to boil over and a few scuffles broke out amongst the ones that were gettin' bored, namely a couple o' Duncan's biker mates. Larry summed up the situation and, bein' a brother in arms, understood where they were comin' from as there were a couple o' real wankers there who thought they could taunt them and get away with it.

It all started when one o' these wankers went about the camp, showing porno photos of a woman flashin' her pussy in various positions.

The biker boys later found out that these pics were of his missus and shone a bad light on the matter. This wanker decided that he was right and they were wrong, so confronted them with a threat. Didn't work! Larry felt embarrassed for his wife as the photos were taken as a personal thing in their own bedroom with the utmost trust.

It was later known that the wife stabbed and killed the wanker at a party. The judge found her guilty of manslaughter and sentenced her to community work for twelve months.

The weird weather persisted for the next day until the Cumulus Nimbus started to roll in. The wind got up and started blowin' a gale.

The far north was right in the path of a tropical cyclone, which nobody was really aware of, not to the extent of the storm.

It was nearin' midnight. The wind was howlin'. Tents were bein' blown over, boats tippin' over, everyone rushin' about tryin' to save their belongings. Larry and Shelly felt they were safe, huddled up in their tent with Sarah sound asleep between them. Their tent seemed to be holdin' up to the storm around them. Just when they thought all was well, there was an almighty gust o' wind. It caught Larry and Shelly's tent and *rrrrip*, a huge hole appeared in the roof of the brand new tent.

The rain was so torrential that everythin' in it, includin' their bedding was saturated within a few minutes. They both scrambled to save what they could before another gust caught the tent and ripped it clean off the site and into the sea. Sarah was the first thing Larry thought of; he grabbed her and put her into the ute. Larry hastily threw all what was left into the back o' it and both piled into the cab.

The wind was horrendous, the ute rockin' about so badly that Larry decided to hightail it to safety. He looked around him; it was like a war zone and most of the families had packed up and fucked off earlier.

The road up and outta the Bay was a mud path. With all the vehicles before them, it had turned into damn near impassable; lucky for Larry, the ol' Vanguard had a limited slip diff and just made it through the farm and on to the metal road, which was not much better, but at least, they got a grip and were soon shelterin' at Kaeo, a small community about twenty kilometres from the beach.

The wind and rain persisted all that day and night.

The following day saw Larry and Shelly head back to Auckland.

They both spent the remainder of the vacation just cruisin' about the home, gardening, and preparing for the following year.

It was a good year for them both, watchin' Sarah growin'. She was such a dear wee baby always smilin' and happy. Larry's business was doin' rather well. He sold the ol' Vangurd and bought himself and Shelly a new Ford.

Life carried on for the next few years, doin' what they both enjoyed. Their relationship was a good one, with hardly a cross word between them. But Larry noticed Shelly was startin' to let her appearance down; not only that, but her duties in the home were also seemingly put on the back-burner.

Larry's business was romping along. Shelly was bored at home.

She was a career girl; hence, she invited a lot of her solo mother and married friends, with babies, to the home, mainly for company, Larry thought. Coming home from work to find these women still in his home at five in the arvo was gettin' to Larry. Shelly had no dinner cooked, bloody babies everywhere, housework not done, washin' piled up, and shitty nappies piled up in the wash house. Nonetheless, Shelly was still as cruised as always. Larry's business bein' so busy, he didn't give Larry a lot of time with his little girl. This was makin' him feel really restless.

Larry's sis Bobby had scored a job in a store in Mairangi Bay.

Bein' central for the East Coast Bays gave Larry the opportunity to duck in there from time to time to have a bite to eat with Bobby on her lunch break.

Bobby worked in the fashion industry and a few of her work mates were like models. One in particular was always on to Bobby to introduce her to Larry, but Bobby made it quite clear that he was a married man and a 'no-go' zone. This woman was of Latin descent, maybe Spanish or Brazilian, thought Larry.

It was a Friday night, and Shelly had invited Bobby and her work mates to a party at their home. It was basically an all-girls affair, so when Larry arrived home after havin' a few beers with his mates, he was confronted with half a dozen gorgeous girls, especially the Latina.

The night got louder as the booze flowed. Larry had the job of chief drink pourer.

In all the years he and Shelly had been together, it had never entered his head to look at anyone else. It was because of the way Shelly had let herself go that prompted Larry to flirt.

He was turning into the hallway from the kitchen, where the drinks were kept. Angel, the Latina, had quite conveniently decided to go take a pee for which the hall was the only access. She caught Larry by surprise as he turned with a glass of drink in each hand. Her arms immediately were around Larry's neck, pushing her body closely to his and placing her moist lips on to Larry's givin' him a long, hard snog. Larry couldn't do a bloody thing. The fruits of his loins started to grow as he felt the mound of her pussy pressing on his cock.

Bobby's voice startled them both.

'Come on, you two,' was her remark. She glanced at Larry with an unapproving look. Angel quickly released her grip and made her way to the dunny. Larry turned and made his way back into the kitchen, his cock as hard as a rock. It was a good couple o' minutes before his rock hard deflated. He topped up what he had spilt, turned to see Shelly walk in wanting to know what the hold up was 'cos the girls were gettin' thirsty.

He could hardly look her in the eye.

Larry continued to meet Bobby for lunch. Angel was gettin' more and more persistent and started invitin' herself along.

It was summer, and the beach bein' only fifty metres away from the shops, it was where they spent most of the time. Angel used this opportunity to tempt Larry with her sensuality—layin' back on her elbows, dressed up to the top o' her legs, her beautiful full breasts stretching her blouse, open to reveal her olive skin and deep cleavage. Larry couldn't keep his eyes off her. This woman was an Amazon goddess.

It was peltin' down with rain; Larry's job was washed out. Wonderin' what to do with himself, he decided to pay Bobby a visit before lunch.

Angel greeted Larry as he sauntered into the store askin' the whereabouts of Bobby. Angel wasted no time in tellin' him she was havin' a sicky, and he would have to take her for lunch instead.

'Pick me up at twelve,' she whispered as she brushed past him. He could smell the perfume wafting up his nostril.

'OK,' he pronounced, hardly believin' he had said it. 'What the fuck am I doin'? he thought as he drove to the pub for an early beer. Come twelve, he was thinkin' really hard about all this, and every time he thought of that kiss in the hallway, his balls started to rearrange. 'Fuck it, what have I to loose?' he asked himself and off he went.

Angel was waitin' for him in front of the store. She was stunning. She swayed over to Larry's ute, swinging her handbag with the utmost sex appeal and hopped in. Larry looked at her in disbelief.

'Where are we goin?' he asked her.

She had no qualms as to what she wanted. She opened the front door to her apartment beckoning Larry inside.

He watched as she walked ahead of him, a rock hard cock protruding from his shorts. She turned as she entered the kitchen and saw the bulge in Larry's shorts.

'I think we're in the wrong room,' she said, putting her hand on his groin, giving it a good rub. All this was too much for Larry. He ripped off his T-shirt and grabbed Angel.

He fumbled with her bra strap, ripped off her top, and tore the bra from her body, and both of them were in utter turmoil. There wasn't time to go to the bedroom. Larry's shorts were on the floor, and Angel's dress and knickers were lyin' beside them. He had never seen a body like that—olive, perfect breasts.

Her tummy shimmered with the sweat from Larry's body. Larry lowered her to the floor. Before they were hardly horizontal, Larry was hard up inside her. He fucked her violently, both o' 'em screamin' and moanin' until Larry felt the hot flow engulf him, both reachin' ecstasy together, before collapsing beside each other.

'Fuck me,' Larry moaned, Angel commenting the same.

Angel didn't bother getting dressed; she made her way into the kitchen, fillin' up the kettle for a coffee. Larry fumbled in his trousers for his fags and proceeded to roll a durry.

He took a long deep drag and focused on Angel pouring the coffee—the deep groove of her backbone, the perfect behind, her beautiful black wavy locks cascading down over her olive shoulders.

.'This just must be a dream!' he thought. It wasn't until she turned and made her way over to him, pressing her warm body on him, engulfing him with a soft and gentle kiss, he realised it was for real.

Angel had an hour for lunch, so as soon as the coffee was over, they made their way to the bedroom, where the most intimate of lovemaking Larry had ever experienced took place.

The weather had lifted by the time Larry dropped Angel back to work. She had given him her phone number, insisting he call her.

Larry went back to his job but couldn't come to grips with work and buggered off to the pub. Wally and Pete were there, a couple of his builder clients. He pondered whether or not to brag about his escapade with Angel but thought better of it. He stayed at the pub until closing at 10 p.m. He was well on the way to oblivion but drove the ten kilometres back home. If the cops had stopped him, he was a gonna for sure.

Shelly didn't mention a thing about why he was late; she just exclaimed that he must have had a good time. That evening, making love to Shelly wasn't the same. He tried to block out Angel, but her face and body haunted him the whole time he made love to his wife.

Larry called Angel that Thursday arvo. Thursdays was boys' night out, and Larry jumped at the opportunity to meet her. The lust between them went on and on and the more he saw of Angel, the less interested he was in Shelly. Shelly sensed somethin' wasn't right with Larry but not once did she doubt his loyalty; she put it down to stress at work. Shelly suggested they go away for the weekend, just the two of them, so he could wind down. They drove to Rotorua for a bit o' relaxing in the hot pools and eatin' out. Larry was tense all weekend and couldn't make love to Shelly the way it was before Angel turned up on the scene.

One Thursday night, after spending until three in the morning with Angel, Larry parked his ute in his driveway. He didn't carry a key to open the door; Shelly always left the door unlocked. This time it was locked.

He pounded on the door yellin' for her to open up. There was no answer.

He turned and made his way back to his ute, hopped in, and decided to head back to Angels. Larry reversed out on to the street, glanced at the house, only to see Shelly standing in the doorway. He made one of the biggest mistakes in his life. He drove off.

All the way to Angels, he could still see Shelly's silhouette in the doorway. He had made his mind up not to go back, but instead of goin' to Angels, he went to Bobby's house. He spilled the whole affair to Bobby, who was understanding but not sympathetic to Larry. She exclaimed to him that Shelly had had a fair idea somethin' like this was goin' on but wiped it out because she couldn't believe Larry would do such a rotten thing to her.

It was soon all out in the open; Shelly was absolutely devastated. Her whole world shattered around her—her dreams of their own home, kids, and family! Larry was an arsehole! How could he just walk out on her and his little girl! That first decision Larry made had definitely changed his life.

Larry continued to see Angel regularly. She would have liked it if Larry had moved in with her, but Larry couldn't do it. What he had done to Shelly was bad enough, let alone moving in with Angel. That would really be rubbing the salt into the wound. Instead, Larry concentrated on his work, fishin', divin', and screwin' Angel.

Their relationship ventured on a few more months. Larry had the taste for freedom once again.

He popped around to Shelly's to pick up Sarah for weekends. Angel was pressurising him for commitment, but after Shelly, he couldn't bring himself to commit to her.

It was the year Larry was to turn twenty-two. Bobby had married a few years before. Her husband was an ex-biker. He and Larry were always the best o' mates. Clive stood a good six foot four, dark and handsome. Larry was already an uncle when their daughter was born. Clive was a dead keen hunter and always down country shootin' deer. The overseas market for wild venison was rapidly growing and in big demand and prices were escalating.

Clive approached Larry on the possibility they both go and have a crack at makin' a few bob huntin'. The pair o' 'em had ventured to Muriwai poachin' fellow deer and had often gone on weekend shoots down country.

Larry got to thinkin' 'bout his life—Angel naggin' at him, and Shelly always pleadin' with him to have another go.

Work was becomin' mundane, and he was startin' to have hassles retrievin' payment from some clients. It wasn't lookin' good for him, so decided to give it a go.

A few of his dive mates had buggered off to the South Island after the Paua and were makin' a fortune.

The ute was packed up and ready to go. Bobby and Clive were sayin' their goodbyes, and Larry was makin' a last final check on the supplies.

He looked up, and who shouldn't be standin' there but Shelly, cradling Sarah in her arms. She had come to say her goodbyes and wish Larry bon voyage. Shelly was always in touch with Bobby, so she knew Larry was headin' off that day. She walked over to where he was muckin' about behind the ute, gave him a kiss on the cheek, and held him in her arms, lettin' him know how much she loved him.

He took Sarah into his arms. A big lump welled up inside Larry's guts; he didn't have a clue what to say. He wasn't goin' to say sorry as he felt if Shelly hadn't let herself go so much, the marriage may have been saved. It was Sarah he felt really shit about.

He popped in to say his goodbyes to Angel at her work and hit the road.

The road south wasn't that busy for a Monday, and they made good time to Hamilton, where they stopped and grabbed a feed o' takeaways. The trip down passed through Rotorua and then on to the Rotorua—Wairoa Road. They were headin' for Murupara, a small Maori settlement, and logging town in the middle of the Kaiangaroa State Forest, and then up the Waiau river, all their permits and licenses up to date The Waiau access was a few kilometres before Murupara. Clive knew o' a family there that were prepared to hire them some packhorses.

It was early morning when the ute trundled into Murupara. It was deathly quiet with misty cloud hangin' in the air. They knew from this that they were high up in the Urewera National Park. Every now and then, a Landrover buzzed past, loaded with guys on their way into the forest for a hard day of loggin'. A truck stop loomed up outta the mist, so Larry and Clive hove to and made their way into the diner. It was a big feed of bacon, eggs, tomatoes, and chips. The meal was so big they only just managed to gobble down the last chip followed by a huge mug o' coffee.

Larry was excited and could hardly keep his mouth shut jabberin' away to Clive about huge stags and big money every now and then stoppin' for a drag on a fag.

It was nearin' 6 a.m., so they headed off in the direction of the farm where the horses were kept. Tryin' to negotiate a fair price for the horses became a bit o' a nightmare as the farmer wanted an arm and a leg for 'em. After a good hour, they finally came to a good deal with the lads makin' off with four packhorses, packsaddles, and riding saddles.

Clive rode the leading horse named Flicka to the head o' the track leadin' into the heavy native bush. Larry was already there and had most of the gear unpacked, ready to be loaded on to the packhorses.

One of them was a big seventeen-hand part Clydesdale skewbald. Every time anyone approached him, his eyes rolled back showin' the whites o' his eyes and his ears lay flat on his head, indicatin' he was a skittery son o' a bitch.

On the other hand, Flicka was about a fourteen-hand part Arab and a beautiful lookin' beast. She was intelligent and all the horses were well bred for the bush, had big chests, and big strong rumps.

The gear all loaded and ready to go, Larry made a final check on the ute makin' sure it was well locked up. It would be there a good week before one o' the lads headed back out with a load o' deer, ready to take to Murupara and the buyer.

Most of the trek in was unobstructed. They made their way through the bush until the track they were followin' opened up on to an ol' farm deserted during the Great Depression. Grassy knolls appeared everywhere—a great place to spot a deer.

Silently they wound their way along the old farm track, rifles at ready at every turn, hoping to see their first deer of the trip. The wind was right up their arses, so any chance of that was fairly unlikely.

The Waiau river wound its way through the thick native eventually spillin' out miles away into lake Waikaremoana, The Sea o' Rippling Waters.

It was a beautiful sight, crystal-clear waters, and deep pools on every bend!

Now and then, they would spot a few big trout down in the depths.

Some o' these holes were six metres deep, but so clear, it seemed to be only a few metres deep.

They were a good three hours into the trek when Clive suggested they stopped for a brew up.

They rounded a bend in the river, swimmin' the horses from one side to the other, makin' their way up a steep bank and over a small point.

On approaching the river again, on the other side, a small spiker was feeding by the river, startled by the sound o' the horses, it scurried off up a bank and into the bush. There, on the edge of the river, was a small knoll covered in grass. This is where they stopped for a break. The ground on the knoll was absolutely covered in deer shit. 'It must be a meetin' spot for them,' Clive suggested.

They later referred to the spot as 'The Knoll'. Across the river a small tributary shot off into a gully, with small river flats on either side. The lads sat there in silence, contemplating the area. It was a good spot to frequent for an early mornin' hunt.

It was approachin' late arvo by the time they arrived at Totara hut. It was constructed of split Totara logs, hence the name. It consisted of four bunks and a fireplace with a couple o' bits o' number eight wire strung from one side to the other, with a griddle plate danglin' from them. These huts were constructed for hunters and hikers by the New Zealand forest service, funded mainly by the government and the fees which were collected from huntin' and hikin' permits.

It wasn't long before Larry had the fire goin' and a brew in the pot. Bein' of high altitude, it was freezing cold. They had encountered a bit o' sleet on the way in after a brief shower passed over.

Just as the daylight was diminishing into the bush, Clive and Larry staggered off up a small creek behind the hut for a bit o' a peek.

There was sign that there was an abundance o' deer. Nobody had hunted the area for at least nine months, so the rangers welcomed the two o' 'em with open arms.

Deer in National parks did a lot of damage to the regrowth in native forests and every now and then had to be culled out, and that's just what the boys' permit was for.

The added bonus, of course, was that they could sell the meat so the animals weren't left to just rot.

The next mornin' the lads were up and out for a hunt before the daylight had a chance to say good mornin'. Clive shot off down river, whilst Larry headed up a tributary off the Waiau, back upstream. He had noticed this as they rode in. It was a good half hour by horseback, so he threw a saddle on the bay and headed off. It was still dark, but the horse had no trouble pickin' its way up the river to where he was headed. Larry tethered the bay and silently crept up the side creek. It was narrow in places but opened up from time to time into small flats. Shingle slides were frequent as he made his way deeper into the bush. The wind was still, but upon a finger test, he found it was behind him. Larry climbed up a bank and made his way along a ridge where he could keep the creek in view. It paid off as stalkin' over a fallen log, he spotted two hinds grazin' on a pepperwood. He went into a crouch. They hadn't got wind of him and went about their feedin'. Larry lifted his 308 and picked up on the rear hind, squeezed the trigger, and dropped it dead. The other hind reared up for an instant, turned, and looked at its mate.

These deer weren't spooked that easy, havin' the whole of the area uninterrupted by humans. Larry thought of droppin' this one as well but thought better of it as he was deep into the bush, inaccessible for the horse, and a long way to carry two deer; besides, it was only the first day and bein' a young hind would make nice eatin' for them both.

Larry felt quite pleased with himself as he gutted and prepared the deer for the carry-out back to the horse.

It was late afternoon by the time Larry arrived back at the hut, threw on the billy, and set about makin' a brew and preparin' for dinner.

Clive was late gettin' back, and Larry was startin' to become a tad worried as it was nearin' nightfall. He fluffed about the cabin pacin' about, wonderin' where the hell Clive was. It got too much for him by the time it was dark, so he ventured outside and fired three shots into the air. It was a signal all hunters did in cases such as this. It gave a position for anyone to zone into in a state of emergency. Another hour went by. Larry was extremely worried by now. He had not heard any return fire from Clive to acknowledge his whereabouts. Larry went back outside. It was freezing cold and around 10 p.m. He pushed a round up the spout and was just about to let rip when he heard a shuffling in the bushes behind the cabin. Larry froze as it sounded like a pig comin' down to the river for a drink. He heard it again, a gruntin' sound; he went down on his knees into a firin' position and waited for it to come into the open. He could just make out the edge of the bush in the dark, but the moon was in the first quarter and shed a little bit o' light. His finger was on the trigger, ready to fire. There was a loud crashin' noise comin' from the bush like the pig had been spooked, and there, in the line o' fire, came Clive, stumblin' out into the open, puffin' and gruntin' like a pig.

'Fuck me, Clive,' Larry was shakin' all over. He could quite easily have shot him but a rule of the bush when huntin' was to always identify your target and by Christ, this had paid off for Clive, let alone Larry.

Clive was absolutely knackered from his ordeal. He couldn't hear Larry's shots because he had walked up a ridge, and into another catchment, and hadn't realised how far he had gone. If it hadn't been for his experience as a hunter, he would have been horribly lost, but he found his way back albeit ten at night.

Larry and Clive lived in the bush for a good three months before they both decided they head back to the city. Clive was missin' Bobby, and Larry was lookin' forward to seein' his daughter. They both loaded up the horses; Clive rode Flicka, and Larry climbed aboard Stonewall, sittin' astride the packsaddle, both with a packhorse each in tow. They had had a good hunt in the time they were there, comin' and goin' every two days, haulin' the deer to the buyer at Ruatahuna.

There were times when either of them couldn't make it back to camp before nightfall, so had to kip down under the stars in the freezing cold nights, curled up in their twenty below sleeping bags, listening to the sounds of the continuous life of the bush at night. It was the most memorable experience for them both.

Larry lay there thinkin', one night, about the day gone by and bloody Stonewall. He had headed off earlier that day makin' for Ruatahuna. Stonewall had been left behind for a good two weeks. He was a huge horse and unless there were more than four deer, he wasn't needed. The day before, Larry had a good hunt and bagged four deer as they scurried up a shingle slide. They had nowhere to go, so Larry just picked them off one by one.

Stonewall was in a hurry to get back to the farm where he came from and didn't waste any time on his way out. Larry rode Stonewall as he could carry four deer and Larry and the smaller mare, who was heavy in foul, carryin' two more.

Stonewall hit the openness o' the ol' farm and broke into a trot. Once through the farm, it was the road out.

Stonewall was by this time cantering along, makin' a beeline for home. Larry was desperately tryin' to slow him down, but it was an utter waste of time. Tryin' to sit astride a packsaddle, with four deer tied to it, wasn't an easy task even to a well-seasoned rider, and Larry just had to hang on for dear life. The closer they got to the public road, the faster Stonewall cantered, eventually breaking into a gallop. Larry could see the washout loomin' up in the distance. He knew there was goin' to be only one way Stonewall would tackle it, and that was to jump. Larry braced himself tightenin' up on the rein, clampin' his legs as hard as he could around the deer. This was also difficult to do as his legs were stretched out each side over the deer. Stonewall reached the washout at full gallop leapin' across the five-metre gap like a superfortress takin' off landin' on the other side as if it were crashin'. The force of the landin' threw Larry forward on to Stonewall's neck.

Hangin' on to his mane, Larry fought to stay on board, but Stonewall was on a mission and wasn't gonna stop for anyone. Larry bounced and bumped around on his neck until eventually, he ended up hangin' on from beneath like a baby monkey clingin' to its mother. It took a good five minutes for Stonewall to shake him loose with Larry crashin' to the ground. Stonewall's front leg kickin' him outta the way and was gone in the distance.

Larry brought himself to his feet, brushin' himself down the mud and bits o' foliage all over him. It took a few more minutes for the mare to catch up.

Larry managed to subdue her and rode her to where Stonewall was, at the gate to his home, the four deer in all positions around him. Larry could have shot him right there, but the look in Stonewall's eyes brought Larry to his knees in laughter.

'What a fuckin' horse!'

Fortunately for Larry, Stonewall behaved himself on the trek home. It was as if he knew what was goin' on, and every now and then, he looked at Larry lettin' out a wet blurt. It wasn't until they stopped halfway for a fag and a bite to eat did Larry see the beauty in that horse, because ol' Stonewall walked up to Larry nuzzlin' him around the neck and givin' him a few nudges to show that he was Larry's companion for life. He was always a skittery horse and by him doin' this was surely a true bond.

Clive and Larry arrived back in Auckland a couple o' days later. They both had a pocket full o' cash, so had hit the piss all the way home, stoppin' at practically all the country pubs, crashin' the night when too pissed to drive. Bobby tore out to meet them when the two o' 'em pulled up outside the house. It seemed like hours to Larry as they kissed and cuddled. Larry had a knot in his stomach thinkin' how good it would have been if he had received the same welcome, and his daughter was there to meet him, but it wasn't to happen because he had fucked up.

The next few weeks went slow for Larry. He had been to visit Sarah a few times, but things weren't good with Shelly. She had told him she was moving down the line and would only be able to visit Sarah every couple o' weeks. Larry would have liked to protest on her decision, but realised Shelly had to get on with her life.

After a couple o' months up and down, visitin' Sarah, Shelly approached Larry about his visits. She had met up with a bloke, wanted her life to change, and requested him not to visit Sarah any more as it was interferin' with her relationship with her new bloke. Larry argued profusely with her and tried to explain that it was his daughter he wanted to visit, not her newfound friends. Larry spent many sleepless nights, pondering over what Shelly had said. He knew he had ruined her life and decided he would give Shelly her way for now so she could get on with it. He had a gut feeling that one day Sarah would look him up, but Shelly would have to keep him informed as to how she was doing and that he could see her once in a while. She agreed.

Larry wasn't workin' because he had a good stash o' cash from the huntin'. He kept thinkin' of his daughter but had to stay focused. He thought of ol' Stonewall and how beautiful animals really were and decided from that moment he would never kill another animal again. In fact, Larry had undergone a transition in his life after livin' in the bush.

It was early seventies and the hippie revolution was on. Viet Nam was an option and love and peace was another.

Larry opted for the love and peace brocure.

He never bothered to contact Angel because he didn't want to commit himself.

It wasn't difficult to get hold o' dope. The new revolution saw every one of Larry's mates smokin' up large. If one wasn't growin it, someone else was.

Piss ups became smoke ups along with booze of course, but a much more passive experience for them all. Make love, not war, and that's just what Larry did. He just couldn't go wrong with the chicks. The experience of makin' love while off his face blew him into a new world when the inevitable crept up on him; he fell in love with his mate's girl. It was so gut wrenchin' for him the fact he couldn't do a bloody thing about it in all respect for his mate.

It was a Thursday night. All the boys had decided to meet at the pub. Larry hadn't got wind of the arrangements and bowled around to his mate's house as they always did on a Thursday. Carl wasn't there, but Barbie was. Larry almost felt nervous and had a lump swell up in his guts.

He was so smitten on her, he almost blushed. Barbie was fuckin' gorgeous—the body to die for, the platinum blond hair, the cutest face one would ever hope to see, the personality Larry just couldn't resist, all of what she was Larry always hoped for. He couldn't get around the fact that Carl took her for granted and cheated on her continuously.

Barbie beckoned Larry inside, Larry askin' where Carl was. What Barbie didn't know was that Carl was about to cheat on her.

After an hour or so of chattin' away, Larry started to feel a bit uneasy as Barbie kept on to Larry how 'spunky he looked that night'. Larry needed a glass o' water and made his way to the kitchen, filled a glass, and turned to find Barbie right in front o' him.

She gently removed the glass from his hand, slid her arms up around his neck, pushed her body hard into his, and gave him the most delicious kiss he had ever experienced. He had never felt the warmth of love in a kiss like this one. Not only that, her body seemed to be alive with electricity as she pushed herself even harder into him.

He could feel her pussy hard against him. It took all of thirty seconds before he was rock hard, Barbie whispering in his ear that she was in love with him and always had been. Larry's whole body went into a state of gel. This feeling he had was a million times better than any dope or whatever the pier could throw at him. His head was spinnin', and his body was tremblin'. How could this be happenin'?. He took her in his arms; the warmth of her was like fire. The more she pushed, the wetter her pussy got until he could feel the dampness through his jeans.

'Make love to me, Larry,' she whispered. Larry picked her up in his arms and carried her into the bedroom. It didn't matter to either of them where they were; they were on another planet, nothing in the universe could stop them now. Larry placed her on the bed and slowly started to undress her, both of them never taking their eyes off each other—first, the blouse and then the bra. Her perfect little breasts were snow white. Larry slowly bent over and kissed them all over, Barbie sucking in deep breaths every time he kissed. Barbie started to remove Larry's shirt; he could feel the love in her hands when she caressed his tanned body, over his rock-hard abs and bodybuilder chest. He slowly undid Barbie's jeans, pullin' them over her perfect behind and down her beautiful long legs. Her panties were next, and, bending down once more, kissed her belly all the way down until he could smell the sweetness of her womanhood. He removed her panties in one sensual motion and opened her legs wide, moving down, kissing her perfect mound. Barbie was sighing and panting, Larry moaning and breathing heavily, this was truly another place where only the two of them could possibly be. Larry moved his body slowly up and on to Barbie. She couldn't wait any longer, pulling Larry into her and inside. Barbie pushed until Larry could go no further, both of them lettin' out little moans as Larry made love to her. She was like velvet, moaning with every motion and soon they were in a whirlpool of ecstasy as they both exploded in to another dimension. This just wasn't real, of all the experiences Larry had had in his twenty-two years, this was mind-blowin'. If this was love, Larry wanted this more than anything life could give him, but the only thing that was in the way was Carl.

Barbie had been Carl's girl since high school. They were an item around town, popular, well loved, and the perfect couple, so it be told!

They lay there in each other's arms, both knowin' full well what the outcome would be.

Larry couldn't sleep that night or the next.

It was the followin' week Larry got a call from Barbie. She had rung to tell him the news that Carl had proposed to be married a week before they had met, but she wanted Larry more than anything.

It was a situation that was eatin' them both up inside. Carl's parents were rich; he had always had the best car, the best of everything, and had only a sister in for a bulk payout when his parents passed. It was a social thing. Barbie's parents were very well off, and she also was from a family of only a brother, so they were in the money as well. Larry was dumbfounded. He didn't know what to say, he couldn't get her face off his mind; it was like she was attached to his eyes.

Barbie wanted to meet Larry at a secret location for a talk. It was the following Thursday, when Carl was out with some o' the boys, in a newly developed subdivision. Larry pulled up to find Barbie there already.

He climbed into her car to be greeted with a beautiful warm kiss. Barbie wanted to continue seeing Larry and end her relationship with Carl.

They made passionate beautiful love again in the front seat and went their own ways. They met on a regular basis for months but nothin' was happenin' as far as gettin' rid o' Carl. Larry kept up the pressure on Barbie, but it was 'technical' because of the social climbin' of the two lots o' parents.

Larry was a Westy, no two ways about that, no matter what scene he was in. Where he was from always stuck out. The scene in the bays was a little different to what Larry was used to, so Larry made a decision and decided to fuck off to Oz and give Barbie time to sort things out between her and Carl.

Carl was quite unaware as to what was goin' on until one evening Barbie visited Larry at his flat on the beach. They had just made love and havin' a chat and a cuddle on his couch when fuck me, the lounge window was wrenched open and Carl climbed in, makin' a track for Larry. Larry just had time to stand up to defend himself when Carl grabbed his shirt pushin' him backwards and over on to the floor.

He was on him like a man possessed, but Larry had had dealings with Carl in the past and knew he could deal to him without a problem. Larry subdued Carl in a few minutes, Carl quietened before Larry did some damage. Larry let him off lightly because he didn't want to make a total fuckwit outta him in front of Barbie. This was the spoon in the puddin' that made Larry decide to call it off.

CHAPTER FIVE

Oz

It didn't take Larry long to pack up his gear and organise his ticket to Australia. He had a few things to sell along with his wagon, tools, etc.

Ol' Tom was rentin' a house with Bobby and young James who had moved in with Tom a few years earlier. He had reached fifteen now and had finished school and moved out of Viv and Ruperts.

The dairy Viv and Rupert had bought had gone to the wall, Viv had got herself pregnant, and Larry had another bro.

Because of all the traumas, it prompted them to move to Oz. Young James had gone with them and finished his schoolin' there.

They moved back to New Zealand and Rupert scored a job at a steel mill in the south of Auckland. James was feelin' his way and wanted to spend some time with ol' Tom. Tom had settled down somewhat and had come to terms with his bust up with Viv and was gettin' on with his life. He was retired now and gettin' the war pension. James was into his music and bashed out 'Wipeout' on his drums relentlessly drivin' everyone bloody crazy. Bobby and Clive had busted up, which was a shock to all as they seemed inseparable.

Bones had decided to go with Larry to Oz, and it wasn't long before they were touchin' down at Sydney. Although Larry had sold practically everything he owned, he only arrived with five hundred bucks. Bones had, fuck, all money, so it was up to Larry to fork out for things.

First stop was the suburb of Waverly out towards the famous Bondi beach. The two o' 'em settled into the Waverly hotel.

First priority was to buy a car to get around in and found a FB Holden out Liverpool way. Unfortunately, it turned out to be a heap o' shit, and eventually, they dumped it on the side o' the road after the cops chased them halfway round Sydney. Bones did the drivin' and managed to elude the cops by duckin' into a private house and hidin' in their garage until the heat went.

By this time, their money was runnin' out. Larry noticed a job scaffoldin, so the two o' them managed to get a start together.

Relyin' on transport was gettin' to the lads and soon the job petered out. With bugger all money, they had to move outta the hotel.

They had bumped into a mate who had been livin' at the Astra hotel in Bondi. Jerry was a Bays boy who had gone to Oz a few months before Larry and Bones. He suggested that he leave the window to his room unlocked so the two o' 'em could sneak in there in the evening without payin' and crash on the floor. This was a godsend for the lads.

A few weeks went by. Larry and Bones were gettin' to the desperate stage with their money. It got that way they were doin' runners from restaurants makin' sure they got a table close to the doorway so they could hightail it in a hurry. One night the three o' 'em were chattin' away when Jerry suggested they fuck off to Cairns. Apparently, there was a lot o' work there and not only that, but it was tropical.

They pooled their money for the fare leavin' Larry with a lousy forty bucks to survive on, but it was OK 'cos they were off to the far north Queensland.

The trip on the train took three days and two nights. They had a ball all the way up. Bones and Jerry got involved in a game of cards, whilst Larry concentrated on scorin' a chick. It didn't take him long, and it was into the dunny for a bit with a young sheila he had met.

Larry wasn't at all interested in cards and when Jerry and Bones asked for a loan to bet with, he was reluctant, but they assured him they would win the money back they had lost. They didn't!

Their opponents were a couple o' Greeks on their way to Mackay to work in the sugar mill. Upon arrival at Mackay, they left the train, but as they passed by Larry, one o' 'em threw forty bucks in his lap, thankin' him for a good game o' cards. They knew Jerry and Bones had borrowed it from Larry and felt sorry for him. Larry would never forget what this Greek had done.

The train pulled into Cairns station around midday. The lads grabbed their gear and jumped off. It was like jumpin' into an oven.

The heat after New Zealand and Sydney was unbelievable and made them all the more excited. A pair o' shorts, a singlet, and sandals were all they needed.

The smell of the tropics wafted up their noses; parrots and all kinds of bird life could be seen everywhere. This was truly a paradise. Larry turned to Bones only to bump into the young bird he had been bonkin' on the way up. What Larry hadn't been aware of was that this sheila was a runaway and was expectin' Larry to look after her.

He didn't know what the fuck he had got himself into. It was a look from Bones that made him decide what to do, and that was to walk away. He never looked back as this young lass stood on the platform, with nowhere to go and nowhere to live. Larry felt like a proper arsehole, but it was bein' 'cruel to be kind,' he told himself.

It didn't take long for the lads to find a place to stay. It was a boardin' house on the esplanade. The landlord showed them to their rooms layin' down all the rules in the process. Breakfast at seven, lunch at twelve, dinner at five on the dot if they wanted them to do the cookin' or else, they could cook their own tucker in the kitchen, which they opted for.

Although forty bucks wasn't much, it was a lot in the seventies.

After a bit of a look around and buyin' a bit o' tucker, they made their way back to the digs. The kitchen was full o' people, much to their surprise as it seemed they were the only ones there.

There were introductions all round and soon food was on the table.

One of the blokes there was the remnants of Hitler's youth army.

Larry thought how young he looked, but he assured them and proved it with his passport and age. He turned out to be a really interesting character, and they talked away till nearly midnight when they all crashed. It took Larry only a few days to find work as a drainer.

There was a huge van park bein' built in the middle o' Cairns, and that's where his main work was.

Months went by. Some of the guys that lived at the boardin' house suggested they all share a big house together. One o' the guys was a con artist Ozzie bloke. Johno was no slug and had bludged his way all around the world. Bones and he became good mates, Jerry stuck to himself, and another Kiwi they had met tagged along. Kev was a hard case Maori fella, and Larry and Kev got on well.

The new pad was a real party house. The next door neighbours were a bunch o' Canadian chicks, and it wasn't long before they were tucked up in the boys' beds after the countless parties.

Just down the road was another house full o' Thursday Island girls. They were always on the boys' doorstep and as hot as hell.

Because it was the seventies, dope was plentiful, and every party was full of it. Larry was the only one in the house that had a job, the rest were all on the bloody dole.

He was startin' to get a bit pissed off with the situation, and to top it off, a house across the road full o' all nationalities, started turnin' up at the parties. Before ya knew it, they had been booted out because they hadn't paid the rent and were all bunkin' down at the boys' house.

All in all, seventeen people were crashin' there; it was turnin' into a dosshouse. Kev was not happy and nor was Larry. Kev had a mate down Blackwater Way, buildin' houses on contract. This is where Kev and Larry headed.

Townsville was such a nice place Kev and Larry decided to have a look around. They had got to know a sheila who worked at a car rental place and was hot, hot, hot. Neither Kev nor Larry let on to the other their intentions. Larry informed Kev he was gonna go for a bit o' a wander round town not lettin' on he was goin' to pop into the car rental.

It was a good half hour before Larry finally got to call in to see Karen.

He couldn't believe it; here was Kev, leanin' over the counter, all lovey, dovey, chattin' up Karen. He had beaten Larry to the jump.

Larry swaggered up to Kev with a grin on his face, Kev turnin' to Larry laughin' out loud. It was a hilarious situation that even Karen saw the funny side. Here she was with two lads hangin' out and made a quick decision that she would go on a double date with both o' 'em.

It was 'Jonathan Livingston Seagull' that the three o' 'em sat and watched, Karen in the middle, with Larry and Kev, each holdin' a hand. Larry felt such a 'Dick'. After the movie, which was the five-o'clock session,

Karen invited them both back to her house for a drink. Whenever Larry left the room for a piss, Kev tried to make a move and vice versa. Karen had a camper van that she wanted to go bush with and invited the two o' 'em along. Kev and Larry looked at each other in total amazement. Neither of them knew what to say, and when Karen went for a pee, Larry and Kev had a quick decision makin' conversation.

Karen came back into the room, Kev makin' a beeline for the dunny, leavin' Larry to spill the beans that they were goin' to head off the next day to Blackwater. Karen wasted no time and had Larry in the bedroom, striped naked before Kev came back into the room. Larry was grinnin' from ear to ear. When it was all over, Larry grabbed his fags and fired up, when, fuck me, Karen called to Kev. It was his turn!

Rockhampton was a bigger city than Cairns or Townsville. As soon as the train pulled up the two o' 'em made a track to the nearest pub for a well-earned beer. The trip down was full o' talk about Karen and what a good sport she was. She had satisfied them both in more ways than one.

By the time they had had a bellyful the last train to Blackwater had already departed. They had nowhere to sleep and to top it off, they were both pissed. Kev noticed a coal train creepin' along at snail's pace and suggested they hitch a ride as it must be goin' to Blackwater where all the coal mines were. Larry didn't hesitate and in their pissed state jumped the train.

It was great sittin' up on top of the coal wagon, with the warm night air blowin' in their faces. The train started to slow after about an hour. Larry could see lights of a station up ahead. Neither of them gave it a thought there could be someone there. The train slowly rumbled through. Larry noticed a bloke watchin' the train trundle by. He looked at Larry perched high on top o' the wagon, with Kev singin' 'Hoki Mai' beside him.

Larry looked at him. It didn't take an instant for him to duck into the office and call up the railway police. Twenty minutes later, the train came to a halt at a siding. The night was deathly still. They heard the sound of dogs barkin' in the distance. They knew then they were in deep shit. Larry was first off and into the long grass beside the track, and Kev right up his arse. They crawled along on their bellies for a good fifty metres all the time crapin' themselves, in case they come across a snake. They hid there in the undergrowth for a good hour before the train eventually moved off. 'Whew' that was a close call. They hadn't a bloody clue where they were, crashin' through the scrub until they finally stumbled across a dirt road. Ten minutes later, they heard the sound of a car approachin'.

It was an ol' FJ Holden. It skidded to a halt as Larry flagged it down.

The driver was a railway worker and had heard about stowaways on the train, but he thought it a great joke and offered them a lift to the highway just up the road. He was half cut from bein' on the grog and just up the road was nearly an hour. He drove like a maniac slidin' on every corner. Larry and Kev had sobered up by then and were shittin'. The driver informed them the highway was gettin' nearer and before they knew it, they were across the intersection and into the scrub on the other side o' the highway. Both the lads couldn't get out quick enough and after bein' pointed in the right direction, headed for Blackwater in the middle o' the night, miles from nowhere.

It seemed an eternity before they heard the sound of a vehicle approachin'. The lights were damn near blindin' them as it got closer and closer. Larry had a sick feelin' in his stomach. This wagon was headin' straight for them and didn't intend stoppin'. Larry yelled to Kev to get the hell off the road as the pickup truck veered off the road in an attempt to bowl them over. There was a small bank beside the road, which the boys clambered up just in time as the truck reared up the bank just missin' the pair o' 'em.

'Bloody arseholes,' they both yelled. They had actually tried to run them down.

Still a bit shaken with the ordeal, they carried on for a couple o' miles until they came to a bridge over a creek, with no water in it. There was a bit of a clearing they could just make out in the darkness.

This is where they decided to stay until morning. About an hour had passed when they heard the dull throb of a road train in the distance. It was headin' their way. Larry was a bit sceptical about flaggin' it down, but Kev was adamant. He sat in the middle of the road until the lights of the big rig appeared over a rise. It got closer and closer until they heard the sound of the gears changin' down until the monster rig pulled up in front o' 'em. The driver just sat in his seat waitin' for one of the lads to approach him. Larry was first there to a greetin' of 'Gidday mate'.

He was a wirey little bloke, black singlet, and an 'Akubra' hat perched on his wisened up head. He informed both o' 'em they were in noman's land and were lucky those blokes didn't run 'em over 'cos nobody would have given a damn.

He beckoned them aboard and drove them all the way to Blackwater, pullin' into town just as the sun was comin' up over dead flat scrub speckled countryside, basically a flamin' desert.

Larry and Kev couldn't thank him enough and bid goodbye as he moved the huge rig off on his way to Emerald, another mining town further inland.

There was already activity around town as all the shift workers from the mines were comin' home and other blokes startin' the day shift. Kev's first priority was to check out his mate and, after a few enquiries, were soon sittin' down at Greg's table, scoffin' down bacon and eggs.

Greg was a Kiwi who had been livin' and workin' in Oz for the last five years and worked on a dragline in one of the many open cut mines in the area. He informed them both that the buildin' had come to an end, and the only work they were likely to get is if they cruised out to the mines to find a job. Greg had a mate who was PR man for a drift mine about thirty miles away. He offered to take them out there as his shift didn't kick off till four that arvo.

After all the bullshit of paperwork, Larry and Kev found themselves unloadin' their packs into draws in their own donga out at the mine's singleman's camp. Their job was to supply props and crowns (timber bracing) for the working faces. Everything was taken down the drift by way of mine cars. The only shift they could get on was dogwatch, midnight till 8 a.m. Larry didn't mind this a bit as the money was big—three hundred eighty dollars a week.

Weeks went by. Larry was enjoying the mining life and also the outback existence he was experiencing with Greg, who was a mad, keen pig hunter.

Larry spent most of his spare time huntin' with Greg. He had an ol' Toyota Land Cruiser he used, pilein all the dogs on and off into the bush.

Larry had done a fair bit o' pig huntin' in his day but nothin' like this.

Bugger me, it was like a walk in the park, absolutely the opposite to huntin' in New Zealand.

A pack o' dogs, most o' 'em Whippet, Labrador cross for the speed, and maybe one or two holdin' dogs, for when the faster dogs ran the mob down. This was nothin' compared to the extreme dense bush of New Zealand Larry was used to. Not only that but most of the pig dogs in New Zealand were bully cross, tough, and aggressive. Not only the dogs but the hunters themselves had to be tough to be able to fight their way through the difficult terrain.

Larry had bought himself a Kawasaki 900 motorbike. It was his pride and joy and was away whenever he could, for a ride.

He often ventured into Blackwater to the pub for a few on his days off. If it wasn't Blackwater, it was Rockhampton.

A couple o' Larry's mates had gone on a pub, crawled up to Emerald. Bustin' for a piss, they pulled over. Kev was with them and merrily pissin' away. He had noticed a stone he had washed clean. It was a vivid green colour. Bendin down to have a closer look, he realised he had washed clean a bloody big Emerald gem stone.

'It must be worth a bloody fortune,' Kev thought. He managed to persuade Larry to lend him his Quaka to ride to Emerald to have it cut and valued. Reluctantly Larry let him have it.

After he had it cut, the bloody thing was worth seven grand. Kev was over the moon. He was in such a hurry, comin' home, he didn't see the cow on the road. He hit it, doin' around seventy miles an hour, totally wreckin Larry's Bike. Kev was thrown clear from the bike and ended up in a paddock unscathed. After walkin' back to the nearest settlement, the local butcher overheard Kev tellin' the publican of his accident. He wasted no time in beltin' down the road with his knives. By the time Kev and the towy had turned up he had cut the cow up and loaded on his truck ready to take back to his butcher shop. When Kev told the story, everyone at the camp thought it a hell o' a joke.

Kev paid Larry the price he had bought the bike for. Larry didn't mind as Kev was OK. Kev headed back to New Zealand with a pocket full o' cash.

Larry had chummed up with an Ozzie bloke who owned a Cooper S mini. The two o' 'em looked bloody ridiculous in this car. With both o' 'em bein' big buggers, it didn't leave much room for anythin' else, but that car could really scamp along.

The Grand Hotel in Rocky was really hummin' with all the miners takin' their R 'n' R.

The pool tables were chocker block with a row o' coins lined up for the next games to take place.

Larry had had a few under his belt and havin' a ball. He had won most o' his games and had held the table for most o' the afternoon.

One bloke set Larry to a challenge: ten bucks a corner. What Larry didn't realise is that this bloke had been sussin' Larry out. He was a hustler.

Larry accepted the challenge, and soon there was a big crowd gathered to watch the event.

It came down to the black and Larry's shot. He lined up not thinkin' about the in off, and it was all over. 'What a bloody idiot!' Larry muttered to himself.

The rule of the day in the Grand was anyone could rechallenge for double or nothin'.

Larry's opponent agreed thinkin' he had it in the bag.

Again, it came down to the black, but it wasn't Larry's shot. He could hardly believe this bloke had missed. Larry sunk the black with the easiest of shots. It was now even, but this bloke wasn't gonna give up and challenged Larry to a fifty-dollar-a-corner game.

He was a lot elder than Larry, and Larry had noticed a wedding ring on his finger and thought why a married man was riskin' two hundred bucks.

The game kicked off with Larry winning by two shots. He couldn't believe it when this bloke doubled or nothin'.

Larry could sense that this guy was gettin' into panic mode but still accepted the challenge.

It took Larry only a short time to clean him up. Four hundred dollars, a bloody lot o' money. To Larry's surprise this dickhead wanted another challenge. Larry thought about it and declined. He wanted the four hundy. The rules were that one could only challenge twice.

Larry held out for his money only to see this bloke break down and start whimperin', statin' how Larry had to give him a chance to win. His wife would kill him when he got home. Larry looked around the bar.

All eyes were on Larry, expectin' him not to back down. Eventually, Larry suggested they change the bet to a dozen beer. It was agreed, and at the end of the game, Larry was sittin on a box o' beer, with all the patrons comin' to him pattin' him on the back, tellin' him what a good sport he was. Larry made a lot o' friends amongst the Ozzies that day. Apparently, this hustler wasn't a popular chappy, and Larry had brought him to his knees.

The thought of a big juicy steak was rumblin' round in Larry's guts.

There was a restaurant in the lounge bar where he headed for a feed. By this time, Larry was well on the way with a slight wobble every couple o' steps. He found himself a seat opposite a loud-mouthed dickhead, who constantly tried to put Larry down. Larry eventually had his steak in front o' him and enjoyin' every bite until the persecution from this punk got the better of him.

It was a straight right fair in his gob that brought the dickhead to the floor. Before Larry knew it, there were two bouncers either side o' him, one grabbin' his steak knife and wrenchin' it from his hand, slicin' a gapin' cut between his thumb and forefinger.

They picked Larry up either side and wrestled him out of the restaurant to the flight o' stairs, which led down to the sidewalk below. His feet were hardly touchin' the ground. Reachin' the stairs, Larry gave an almighty shove with his right arm and sent the bouncer head first on to the footpath below, grazin' a big hunk o' skin off the side o' his face. Larry felt a hand on his back and before he knew it, he was in the gutter with three arseholes bootin' the crap outta him. It was a relentless hiding for a good three minutes.

Larry couldn't feel a bloody thing and started to laugh as the bouncers made their way back up the stairs. They turned to Larry in dismay; they had left him there for dead. Larry rose to his feet. The bouncer who he had shoved down the stairs came at him, but Larry was waitin' for him. The bouncer hesitated when he saw the look in Larry's eye and thought better of it. Larry vowed to them he would be back to finish them off after he had his hand stitched up.

It wasn't long before the whole camp knew what had happened to Larry, with all the boys backin' Larry. It wasn't a good look for a bunch o' bouncers to beat up on one bloke. They all vowed to get back on 'em the followin' weekend.

A couple o' locals knew the bouncers to have a few beers at another pub around the corner from the Grand and that's where Larry's mates and he were waitin'. Word had also got around Rocky that there was to be a big rumble goin' down.

Larry sauntered up to the bar. He could feel a sense of anxiety in the air. Everyone was checkin' the other out as no one knew who Larry was except the bouncers.

The barmaid pulled Larry a Schooner as he leaned on the bar, checkin' out the scene.

There were a few guys playin' pool, a couple playin' darts, and a couple o' tables scattered about with blokes sittin' drinkin'. Larry and his mates had a plan.

They were all there but scattered about tryin' not to be conspicuous except three, who were makin' it quite obvious they were lookin' for trouble. This was a plan to take the attention away from Larry.

A good hour went by until, there, passin' the window, Larry saw one o' the bouncers. He was with a bloke he hadn't seen before. Larry waited for them to enter the pub. The stranger entered with another bloke he hadn't seen before, followed by the bouncer.

The two strangers stopped and spoke to the bouncer turning and lookin' directly at Larry. The pub somehow became deathly quiet. Larry turned and ordered another beer, the four he had already had just gettin' him in the mood. All in all Larry had eight mates to back him up, if, more than the ones he was after turned up. It appeared to Larry that this was goin' to be the case.

There was a tap on his shoulder. Larry swung around to be confronted by the two strangers. He was ready for whatever they dished out, but after they had introduced themselves as Police Detectives, the situation changed suddenly. They made it quite clear to Larry that if he intended causin' any trouble to think twice about it.

They had police in position outside the pub, waitin'. 'Those low, down, gutless fuckin' arseholes had gone to the bloody cops because they were too gutless to have a go,' thought Larry.

The Ds left. Larry's mates came over to where he was standin', wantin' to know what it was all about and were all gutted. They were lookin' forward to a good arvo, especially the three actin' as troublemakers. These blokes were brothers and followed the circus around as prize fighters.

The afternoon went by with the bar fillin' up with blokes, all wantin' to get a look in at what had brought a bit o' action into their lives.

The trip home in the Cooper S was goin' along just fine until just before the gorge. It was a winding stretch o' road for a good five miles.

Some o' the young guys at the mine earned huge money as fitters and turners, electricians, mechanics, and could afford to buy expensive cars. One particular young seventeen-year-old had purchased a GTHO Falcon—one of the fastest cars on the planet. He was right up the Coopers arse as they entered the gorge, but this bloody Cooper was just too good for it through the winding stretch of road. It wasn't until the straight road loomed up that the HO blatted past the Cooper. What amazing little cars these were!

The HO disappeared into the distance. Larry estimated he must be doin' at least 150 miles per hour.

He was absolutely devastated a few weeks later when the whole camp went into mourning for that young man and four of his mates, after a head-on with a Valiant V8 fully raced Charger.

They both approached a slight rise estimated to be doin' well over 140 miles per hour.

The driver of the Valiant was impaled by his steering wheel through the backseat of the car. The Charger ended up half its length. The GTHO ended up in a U shape.

Six young men died that day.

Weeks went by. Larry thought a lot about Sarah, his family, Angel, Barbie, Shelly, and good ol' New Zealand. He decided it was time to head home.

It had been more than a year since he had arrived in Oz, had enjoyed every minute of it, and vowed he would return again one day.

CHAPTER SIX

Good Ol' Enzed

Larry took in the awesome and the wild west coast as the DC ten winged its way over the Manukau heads. He was in total awe of the lush green farmland and dense native bush of the Waitakere ranges. This surely is paradise on earth. He was glad to be back home.

The jet gently bounced down on to the runway at Auckland's international airport. It all seemed fairly insignificant compared to Sydney, but this made Larry feel even better as he knew what was beyond.

The first thing he wanted to do was contact Shelly to see how Sarah was. It was not a good idea. Shelly had remarried, and her newfound hubby had claimed Sarah as his own. Shelly was not the woman he had once known; she had turned vindictive and refused Larry any contact whatsoever and threatened court action to obtain a restraining order against him. Larry was devastated. He had no idea Shelly would turn that way; maybe her new hubby had a lot to do with it. The only hope for him now was that Sarah grew up with an attitude to look him up one day but also vowed he would always try to contact Sarah in the hope he could see her.

Larry hadn't told his family he was coming home. It was a tough decision deciding whom to visit first.

Katrina's life with her husband had come to an end after trips to Italy and finally, Australia. She had moved back to New Zealand and was livin' at Waiuku with her young son, where Viv and Rupert were. Chad, Larry's youngest bro, was nearly at school whilst James had scored a job with a local contractor.

Ol' Tom had moved in with Katrina and Bobby, who had rented a house there.

Larry had rented a Datsun 120 Y at the airport. Viv was busy in the garden as Larry drove into her driveway. Viv couldn't believe it; her big boy had come home! It wasn't long before the whole family knew soon and were all at Viv and Ruperts, includin' ol' Tom who had come to terms with Viv and Rupert and were all good mates.

The booze was flowin' and the ol' radio gram beltin' out Kenny Rodgers, the Stones, but the favourite was Neil Diamond. Larry had a few secrets tucked up his sleeve, and what the family didn't know was that he had smuggled a block o' hash through the airport.

Larry's family were very close, especially now that they were all elder, apart from young Chad. It was a hell o' a joke that he had smuggled the hash and after a meetin' in the dunny, all havin' a toke and were off their trees. Rupert and, of course, Chad, were the only ones that were straight. They had a ball. Rupert was a very nonchalant bloke and although he was straight, joined in on the fun.

Larry really felt elated the fact Tom and Viv had a good rapport with each other and also the fact Rupert was an accepting sort o' bloke. This had brought the family together again and after everythin' that had gone down, they were there together to welcome Larry home. It was truly a fantastic feeling for them all.

Waiuku was a booming steel mill town, with all walks o' life streamin' there for the big money. The fact o' this turned the place into a real party town. Young single men and women were all over the place, and this was just the bee's knees for Larry. He managed to score a job at the mill after only a few days. Larry absolutely loathed it. Here he was trapped in a flamin' steel mill sweepin' bloody floors.

He had met up with a Scottsman who was fresh from the homeland and bloody hard to understand in his broad Scottish accent. It was him and Larry that had the sweepin' duties. They both had a good rapport with each other and after the first day, it was into the pub for a coldie.

Neil and Larry were interested in one thing, and that was drinkin', smokin' dope, and women and believe it or not, Waiuku had it all.

Larry only lasted another couple o' days at the mill before he landed a job with his bro, James.

James had earned himself a reputation as a drummer in one of the local bands, and of course, they played at various gigs around the town throughout the weekends.

This was a haven for all the gorgeous girls, which attracted an entourage of single guys.

Bein' the seventies, it was alternative ethnic wear for the sheilas and jeans, T-shirts and leather jackets for the guys.

Because there was a cross section of people anything went.

The dope flowed, the booze flowed, and sex was everywhere.

Neil and Larry were right in the midst of it and went crazy.

There was so much goin' on, Larry was gettin' to the stage where he didn't give a fuck about anything just as long as he could get pissed, stoned, and fuck as many women as he could, and he was very successful in all departments.

James's band had folded, but he had got together with a couple o' his muso mates and formed another band. It was such a great band that every gig in town belonged to them, consequently attracting a huge followin' and with that plenty o' scraps happenin' at most venues.

There were the hippie types smokin' dope, the juice freaks guzzlin' beer, and the blokes into the whole hog into the scrappin'.

Larry tried to keep a low profile, but there were times when the inevitable happened and found himself nursin' wounds the next day, not that the other blokes came off any better.

The months ticked over. Larry had just about doped, drunk, and screwed himself out. His mind started to wander back to the Northshore and Angel. He had bumped into a mate from the Bays who knew where Angel was living, so decided one sober Sunday to look her up.

She had a quaint wee flat on the shore in a block of two. Larry hesitated at the front gate tryin' to anticipate the reception he might get. It had been more than two and half years since he had any contact with her and felt he might have burnt his bridges, but when the door opened and he saw the look on her beautiful face, he knew then all was well.

Larry spent a good couple o' hours with her chatterin' about what they had both been up to.

Angel had a couple of relationships but went by the way as she explained to Larry she couldn't get him off her mind.

Larry said his goodbyes at the door and left. Drivin' home he could hardly believe he hadn't coaxed her to the bedroom. He had got into such a scene in Waiuku, he thought maybe it's because he wanted to settle down and for some reason had a lot o' respect for Angel.

The followin' week kinda dragged by Larry thinkin' all the time what it was like with her before he left for Oz. He went about his work gettin' stuck in diggin' drains and pourin' concrete.

Come Friday, he gave Angel a call. She could hardly wait for Larry to turn up that night.

Larry arrived at her door with a bottle o' red wine and a dozen beers.

It was nothin' like the week before when they were both feelin' their way. Angel beckoned him inside and proceeded to open the wine and give Larry a beer. On went the stereo to the sound of 'Bread'—Angel's favourite. The atmosphere in that room absolutely reeked of sex. Larry tried to ask himself if it was all about that, or was it he had burnt himself out in Waiuku and was searchin' for a relationship.

The evening flowed by, Angel startin' to feel the effects o' the wine. She staggered out to the kitchen to grab another beer for Larry and a glass o' wine. Her favourite song was playin' as she entered the lounge. She placed the beer and wine on the coffee table and started to dance. Angel was wearin' a pair o' skin-tight stretch pants and a boob tube her breasts pushin' the material to damn near rippin'. Her body started to writhe with the music, throwin' her head back, every now and then, sendin' the sexiest of looks towards Larry. He could feel his loins startin' to move. The more she danced, the harder he got. She was definitely a goddess—her perfect body, the hair, the look in her eyes. She spun around in a swirl, at the same time liftin' her boob tube up and over her head and flicked it at Larry. Her breasts hardly moved but just banged back to where they were. To Larry, they seemed to be bigger, but whatever, they were perfect.

Angel continued to writhe and twist until finally her slacks were on the end of her foot bein' flung directly at Larry, him grabbin' them and flickin' them outta the way as he didn't want to miss one bit o' the show. Her panties were so tiny, just covering her black mound.

By this time, Larry was rock hard. Angel went on her hands and knees and crawled towards Larry with her eyes fixed directly at Larry's bulge. By the time she had reached him, Larry had his shirt off.

Angel slid up his legs and started to bite his rock hard through his jeans. Larry wasted no time to down trou. She took it in her hand and started to caress it with her mouth. Larry was beside himself his head to the point of explodin'. Up and down his legs, he could feel the firmness of her breasts slidin' with the sweat from her body.

She slid all the way up and lay on him pushin' her pussy on to Larry until he was all the way.

This wasn't sex, Larry kept thinkin'; this is somethin' else. What was it with this woman and what was she doin' to him? She was not human, she was from outta space. Everything about her was perfect. Her hair, her face, her body, her breasts, her arse—she was a goddess.

It seemed like an eternity. Larry was sure she was tryin' to get his whole body inside of her, to engulf him. She pushed and pushed, sweat pourin' from them both. Larry was goin' crazy. Angel screamin' and yellin' until all seemed like he was floatin' away. It wasn't until Larry felt her nails rippin' into his chest as she finally succumbed to the ecstasy, Larry's head was spinnin' as he gave her his all.

This just wasn't something that happened. Larry couldn't move.

Angel just lay there as if dead. The music had stopped; it was dead quiet apart from the deep breaths they were both inhaling.

Larry tried to get his head around it all. He put his arms around her and held her tight, she returning the same. He moved to stroke her hair, which was like the black of the night, with stars dancing all over it, the smell of her perfume, and the warmth of her body restin' on him. She lifted her head and stared into him, her eyes like black pearls. Her eyebrows like they were painted on to her forehead, her full lips with the telltale smattering of lipstick still apparent, glistening in the low light of the side lamp. Angel slowly reached closer, her lips touching Larry's with so much passion. Larry could feel something overwhelm him as tears welled up in his eyes.

Angel looked up, her eyes glistenin' with the tears startin' to flow in hers. Larry held her closely cradling her head on his shoulder. They lay there for a good twenty minutes, not sayin' a bloody word.

As Angel rose up from Larry, her eyes were gushin' tears. She was the first to speak, tellin' Larry how much she loved him and wanted to be with him for the rest of her life. Larry didn't know what to say as he was well aware he was most definitely in love with her but was reluctant to let her know that directly. He needed a fag and a drink to think about what had happened.

There was a knock on the door. Larry and Angel scrambled for something to put on, Angel going to the door, opening it just far enough to see who was there. It was the bloody neighbour asking Angel if everything was OK as they had heard a lot of screamin'.

'Oh,' was all that she pronounced and closed the door. She turned towards Larry with her hand over her mouth in embarrassment.

Larry was already halfway through laughing. They fell back on to the couch entangled in each other's arms, giving passionate kisses.

They made love again just to be defiant.

Larry stayed the weekend with Angel, goin' for drives, movies, out for dinner, just a full on weekend of romance.

The week dragged on by. Larry was lookin' forward to the next weekend, in fact, every weekend for the next few months.

The lights were low, the music soft, and they had just made love. Larry had Angel in his arms, all seemed total bliss. Larry felt that his relationship with Angel was startin' to go places. He opened his mouth to speak but was cut short by Angel.

It was a decision that he didn't have to ponder over.

Angel had asked him to move in with her, and he accepted.

CHAPTER SEVEN

The Straight and Narrow

It was peltin' down with rain when Larry moved his gear to Angels.

He felt good about it. It was a new chapter for him, and he did feel like settlin' down.

He had made a few bob in Waiuku, and Angel had some cash stashed away.

Larry got stuck in doin' construction work. He had contacted a few o' his past clients and managed to get work. Fortunately, there was a building boom happenin' and soon he was cruisin' about in a new wagon.

Angel carried on with her work as a beautician at a local chemist shop.

Larry's life had certainly changed. It seemed all he was doin' was bloody well workin, apart from the odd trips down to the country for a break.

Angel wasn't the Shelly type, in fact, the flamin' opposite. Whenever Larry wanted to get away with the boys fishin' or divin', it became an issue, so slowly he pulled himself away from what he really loved.

Angel always wanted a baby. Larry wasn't at all keen on this. The fact that after what had happened to Sarah, he would much rather wait until the relationship was rock solid.

Eighteen months later, Angel dropped the clanger, she was pregnant. Larry couldn't figure how the hell this had happened, but Angel was so obsessed with havin' a kid, she stopped takin' the pill, unbeknown to Larry. Although he was delighted, he had a bad feeling about Angel the fact she had been deceitful.

Kenny was a handsome little boy with thick, jet-black hair, big brown eyes, and chubby. Larry loved him to bits. Angel was a good mum, but as Kenny got to six months and was crawlin', he became a bloody handful; into everything he could get his hands on.

All this was wearin' Angel down, and the only real break she had was when she got to do the shoppin' on a Friday night.

Larry didn't go with her, so stayed and babysat Kenny.

Angel's way to give herself a break was to put Kenny in a playpen for most of the day. He hated it, so when Larry was there on his own with his son, he let him go for it. Round and round the house he went, flat out like there were millions of calories to get rid of, standin' at the coffee table bashin' away at it like a drum. Larry loved it, and most of the time fired up a joint, cranked up the stereo and let him go, but still keepin' a close eye. By the time Angel got home, he was plum worn out and after a change of nappies, he was into bed and fast asleep.

Larry had met a few local blokes who used to gather after work at the local. This was important to Larry as he often picked up a few good contracts.

He was havin' a ball. All the boys were there for a few coldies after work. Jokes were flyin' in all directions, everyone crackin' up, each takin' turns around the table, and of course, they were always the ones that held the floor. Larry wasn't too bad a joke teller, but he couldn't compete with some o' the guys that seemed to have a relentless barrage.

Murphy was walkin' down the road with his mate.
He came across a mirror and gazed down into it.
He yelled to his mate.
'Hey, Paddy, come over here, won cha?'
'What is it Murphy?'
'Who's dis in the mirror?' asked Murphy.

Paddy asked him to move outta the way and gazed down into the mirror.

'Well, it's me, you bloody idiot!'

Larry and all the boys laughed like fuck, all takin' swiggs o' beer in between.

The time ticked by, with everyone gettin' well on the way. Some o' the boys started to make their way home. The music on the juke box blurtin' out was just an excuse for another round, then another.

It was nearin' eight o'clock and by this time, only half a dozen blokes were left includin' Larry. One of his mates started yellin' at Larry to look out the window. Larry couldn't believe his eyes. There, standin' at the window was Angel with Kenny on her hip bashin' like fuck on the window. Larry knew he was in deep shit now. Angel kept beckoning him outside. But Larry stood defiant. He was so embarrassed in front of all his work mates.

Angel left and headed home. Larry hung about for another beer and left.

When Larry walked inside his home, he saw another side of Angel that really frightened him.

Her eyes were like ebony fire, her face with a look that could kill, the veins in her neck bulgin' like corrugations on a dirt road.

He had fucked up big time.

Larry appeared like a little puppydog for the next week. Angel was layin' down the law, and he didn't like it at all but said nothin'.

He carried on with his work, diggin' drains and layin' concrete. He still stopped off for a few but made sure he was home before dinner. Kenny was what Larry looked forward to and played away with him until he wore himself out, and Larry put him to bed.

The relationship was goin' nowhere, ever since the night Larry was made a fool of himself. The lovemakin' was gettin' less and less. Angel complained whenever Larry wanted a bit and when it did happen, the love between them wasn't there.

Although Larry made a mistake that night, Angel also had issues with her life. This wasn't what she really expected. Larry had a taste of relationships with Shelly and half-pie knew what commitment it involved, but Angel was missin' all the glitz and glamour of her job. Larry had noticed it months before but didn't expect things to turn sour.

Larry kept thinkin' if he had a different career, then he and Angel might have got on a lot better. A collar and tie job was what she would have liked Larry to have. She was used to all the social scene, but Larry was into construction and felt because of this, they were really like chalk and cheese. There was no way they could live the rest o' their lives together.

Larry was kickin' himself because o' the night at the pub but felt a few with the boys was OK as long as it didn't become a habit.

He was still in love with Angel but more for her beauty than her nature.

Larry and Angel were startin' to argue more and more, each findin' little faults in each other.

One Saturday, he told Angel he was goin' down to Waiuku to see his mum and asked if she would like to come only to get a rebuff tellin' him she couldn't be bothered with his family right now.

Larry was deeply hurt at this and headed off on his own. Viv was really happy to see him and after spending a good couple o' hours with her, he popped down to visit ol' Tom. Tom had moved into a house with Katrina, who had bought herself a small business. Bobby had met up with a bloke and had fallen in love. They had rented a house together with her daughter and young son.

Bobby and Len were right into parties and a good time.

Her new man and she were like they were joined at the hip, both liking exactly as the other. Larry met up with ol' Tom down at the local for a few and a bit o' a chinwag, reminiscin' about the good ol' days.

Larry tried to explain to Tom about his situation at home with ol' Tom givin' the best advice he could, tellin' him to make sure if he decided on anything, no one got hurt.

Bobby and Katrina barged into the pub. Larry felt really proud as they were both beautiful lookin' women, vibrant and devoted to their family. Larry was so excited he bought a round of drinks for them all.

The afternoon cruised on by. It was great, spendin' a bit o' time with his family, and soon their table was full of all his sisters' friends, all jokin' and laughin'.

Ol' Tom had just about enough and decided to retire back home leavin' Larry with his two sisters.

Ol' Tom had pulled back a lot with his drinkin' and only popped in for a few in the arvos.

Bobby's new partner arrived after a day out with his mates, attendin' a footy game. They were all in a happy mood and suggested everyone return to their house for a party. Larry was a bit sceptical as he really should be makin' his way back to Angel and Kenny, but after a few words of advice about drivin' pissed, ended up back at Bobby and Len's.

Len was a good bloke, and he and Larry hit it off. He was a man's man and enjoyed a good hard day's work and a few beers.

Only a little fellow, but, all the same, not a pushover. The evening really got into the swing of it, people comin' and goin'—married couples, boyfriends, and girlfriends—the ol' stereo bashin' out all the latest songs of the time. It was nearin' closin' time at the pubs and before ya knew it, the place was packed spillin' out on to a huge deck in the backyard.

It was a beautiful evening, full moon and not a breath o' wind.

Bobby and Len lived in the country just outside o' town, so it wasn't a problem to crank the ol' stereo to full tit, everyone dancin', and drinkin'. The ol' weed came out, and the party was in full swing.

Larry noticed a sheila who had come in from the pub; she was a mate of Katrina, and Larry couldn't keep his eyes off her.

She was dressed in a sarong and a muslim top, vibrant, both in looks and personality. Her face was full o' mischief, short cropped blonde hair, green eyes that danced as she spoke, a strong straight nose, and lips a bloke wanted to kiss. She wore a scarf around her neck, which reached right to her feet, just touchin' the top of her leather sandals. She danced and bounced around like a gypsy, her mischievous smile and eyes darting a glance at Larry every time he looked up at her.

'Fuck me,' thought Larry. 'What next?' He couldn't resist it and made his way over to where she had sat down.

Larry couldn't believe how well they got on. She was full of fire, just what Larry needed to pull himself out o' the rut he and Angel were in. Larry talked and talked his head off to her both o' 'em fascinated with each other. She had a story to tell and so did Larry. They hit it off like they had been together for ever and before they knew it they were both gazing into each other's eyes tryin' to find what the other had in mind.

He had made a phone call to Angel lettin' her know that he wouldn't be home till the next day, which made him feel a little more relaxed.

The hippy revolution had got to Larry when he was in Oz. Cruisin' about, dreamin' about alternate lifestyles, a house in the country, big veggie garden growin' dope, the whole scenario appealin' to him, but never, though, he could meet anyone he could relate to on this until now.

Larry had a deep gut feelin' that if for any reason he was to get to be with this woman, his life would turn around, and he could be what he had always wanted to be. She enjoyed a few beers and a dak, smoked the same rollies Larry smoked, and loved to live in the country and the great outdoors. She was vibrant and bloody good fun.

The more he looked into her eyes, the greater the lust became, only to be broken when James entered the party after playin' a gig at the local.

Larry was so pleased to see him that he left what could have been a dangerous situation.

The party rolled on into the early hours. Larry spent most of his time between James and his newfound friend and come daybreak and drunk as a skunk, Larry had succumbed to all and crashed out on the couch.

Larry gave Bobby and Len a hand to clean up and made his way back to the shore.

Angel was OK when he arrived home and little Kenny with outstretched arms to greet him. The following week went by, the same ol' humdrum. Angel was back to her naggin' which was drivin' Larry insane, but he kept his cool.

Saturday came, and Larry headed off to work. All week he had been thinkin' of the chick he had met at Bobby's, so instead of workin', he headed down to Waiuku. He couldn't stand the thought of spendin' a Saturday arvo in suburbia.

He went straight to Bobby's house to find her, and Len was already havin' a few beers in the early afternoon sun. Some of Len's mates were there and ol' Tom. Larry felt like he was home amongst them all and even felt better when Bobby told him Katrina was comin' round for a drink and bringin' her mate with her. Larry asked Bobby who her mate was, and Bobby explained to him it was the sheila he had spent the evenin' with, the week before. 'You know, Josie, the hippie bird,' with a grin on her face.

Bobby knew Larry was miserable with Angel. Things hadn't really worked out for him. His life wasn't him at all. She also knew Angel wasn't the girl for him; after all, she had worked with her in the past, tried to warn Larry, but Angel, bein' a goddess, had lured him in. The whole family, in fact, had tried to persuade Larry against gettin' involved. They all knew Larry had always been a good partner, always there for them, a good provider, and understanding.

He and Angel were a complete mismatch. The blood ran from Larry's face; in fact, he felt a little embarrassed as he was dressed only in his work gear—a pair o' shorts, T-shirt, and boots.

Although he was dressed this way, Larry was a fair stamp o' a man.

His hard job had given him one hell o' a physique.

It seemed like bloody hours before Katrina and Josie turned up, all the time Larry guzzlin' a few to ease the nerves.

He kept askin' himself why he was like this. He never had a problem in the past meetin' women, it was second nature to him, but for some reason, Josie was special. Maybe it was because she was so much like him.

Katrina and Josie arrived later in the arvo, Josie dressed in the usual batik skirt and blouse, her head adorned by a colourful bandana.

She seemed to bounce on to Bobby's deck where they were all sittin' in the sun.

She looked directly at Larry, expressin' how it was good to see him, Larry returnin' the same.

By the time it was evening, the few drinks had turned into a BBQ, and some of Bobby and Len's fiends had arrived with a few more crates o' Lion Red beer. Larry and Josie were hittin' it off big time.

He hadn't a clue where he was when he opened his eyes. He was really warm and cosy. He heard a slight sigh and felt an arm slide around his waist. He was in Josie's bed. What had he done? He gathered immediately that he had got so out o' it, he had wound up at Josie and spent the whole night, makin' love to her.

Larry felt like a right prick for not lettin' Angel know where he was.

She would have been beside herself not knowin' his whereabouts.

He rolled over to face Josie, her green eyes luring Larry right into her. He kept on rollin' until he was on top of her and inside. They were both still half cut from the dope and booze. She drew him right inside until he could go no further and lay there gazin' at each other, feelin' all the emotion of lovemakin'.

The whole day was spent in the bedroom, stereo blastin'.

Larry gazed about the room. He could detect the smell of musk in the air from the incense burnin', the batik rugs and tapestry, the pot plants, the scarfs adorning the wardrobes and doors, the crocheted bedspread. The whole room was a harem.

Larry felt he was in another place; he was so excited, he never wanted to leave, and he didn't.

He had remembered what ol' Tom had said to him about hurtin' people but this went out the window as he was never goin' to give up this woman although he hadn't a clue what she was at or anything about her. This was it.

The following week was devastatin' for Angel because of Larry's incompetence, it was left to Viv. Angel had called her askin' if Viv knew his whereabouts and of course, had to do a lot o' explainin' on Larry's behalf and wasn't at all pleased with it.

In fact, the whole family were filthy on Larry for bein' so irresponsible.

They all knew his situation but thought he could have handled it a bit better.

Katrina felt for Angel. She got on well with her as they were both into the fashion scene and invited her down to stay a night or two to try and console her grief.

Angel and Kenny arrived at Katrina's two weeks after Larry refused to go home.

He and Josie were head over heals in love with each other and quite frankly didn't give a fuck what anyone thought.

Angel had somewhat cooled down and had contacted Larry to ask him if he wanted to see his son, which, of course, he jumped at.

Larry and Josie pulled up outside Katrina's early in the evenin' to pick up Kenny.

Katrina had a couple o' her friends there havin' a few drinks.

Larry entered the lounge to see young Kenny with a big grin on his face, happy to see his daddy. He picked him up and gave him a big cuddle. He heard a commotion outside where Josie had been waitin' in the car. It was Angel havin' a go at Josie.

She had had a few to drink and dutch courage, so had gone to Josie to have a chat, which ended up with Josie gettin' a slap and a glass o' wine in her face.

Larry understood how she must have felt, and also, Josie couldn't retaliate because she had understood her as a woman and how she would have felt in the same instance. Josie was a pacifier and didn't like confrontation and handled everything superbly.

Angel didn't want to keep Kenny with her. When he returned the next day, she informed Larry she was gettin' on with her life, and that he was the one who should bring him up. She had met a few guys the night before. Larry figured that anyway. She was stunnin' and the news didn't take long to travel that there was a new gorgeous babe in town. This drew out all the single blokes who made a beeline to Katrina's, all pushin' and shovin' to see who would be the first to fuck her.

Angel was bitter and didn't waste time in shackin' up with a young bloke three years her junior.

Three weeks went by. Larry was havin' a ball with Kenny, and Josie treated him as if her own although she had two kids herself.

They just all slotted in with each other as if they had always been a tight-knit family. The whole atmosphere in that home was so cruisey, never any cross words, and heaps o' love.

Angel had burnt herself out. The young guy had finished with her along with a few others. She had vented her frustration and wanted to have Kenny back and get back into a normal life again.

Larry thought of contesting custody for Kenny. He was so happy in Josie's home, and Josie's kids were so wonderful to him. Josie and Larry had a good talk and decided against it, so Angel went back to the shore with Kenny.

All the finances were sorted. Larry went back and forth to the shore to finish off a few contracts he had.

Larry managed to score his ol' job, back at the contractin' mob he had worked for before he moved in with Angel.

Josie and Larry were out on a night in to the town. Viv had obliged by havin' the kids for the weekend, so they were free to do and go wherever. Larry still had the ute and after stoppin' off at a few pubs here and there, decided to head for the shore and Albany pub. They had a box o' Lion Red cans and a bag o' dope to help them on their way.

Josie decided that she would do the driving, and Larry, feelin' a little pissed, gave her the wheel.

When she went around a corner, Larry told her to slow down a tad because it had been rainin' a little. The road was a little greasy.

Around another corner when Josie drove, Larry yelled to slow down, but it was too late. The ute slid to the right, then to the left, up on two wheels thumpin' back down only to shoot across the road, mountin' a bank, screamin' along the side o' it for a good twenty metres, finally flippin' over twice in mid air, and crashin' down on to the road. Larry grabbed Josie just in time as she flew across in front o' him before skiddin' along on its roof. He could feel the rough surface of the road bubblin' on his arm as it slid a good fifty metres comin' to a halt just before a drop down into a creek.

'Jeeesus,' thought Larry. The roof was flattened so much there was only enough room for him to squeeze out and drag Josie to safety.

What a fuckin' mess! Larry's tools, shovels, pipes, bags o' cement were strewn all over the road.

Bein' a long weekend, the roads were busy with all the traffic comin' and goin'. Larry thinkin' how lucky was that with a lull in the traffic just as they spun out. If there had been a queue approachin' there would have been absolute mayhem.

The cops didn't take long to turn up, but before they did, Larry grabbed the box o' piss and hurled it into the creek; he then grabbed the bag o' dope and stuffed it down around his balls. It made him look a little abnormal but better than wastin' it and also bein' caught. Josie suffered a cut in her arm and was shocked.

The ambulance didn't take long, and soon they were both whisked off to a hospital, the whole time Larry feelin' a little conscious of the bulge in his crotch. All the women that he spoke to wanted to gaze down at what must have seemed a whopper.

Josie had a small car, and after a good discussion, they decided to pack up and get the fuck outta Auckland and head north.

CHAPTER EIGHT

Veggie Gardens and Bread

Kerikeri, a small fruit growin' area, was a quaint little town to the north o' Pihia in the Bay of Islands.

Larry and Josie had rented a cottage on an apple orchard right in the middle o' the town.

Work was scarce, and although they had a little money, it was not enough for them to survive for long. Angel had cleaned Larry out through the courts and had bought herself a unit with the proceeds.

Things were gettin' grim after a month with no work.

Larry got wind of a house for rent on a thousand-acre sheep and cattle farm. It was a big ol' villa which had been moved up from Auckland and needed a good paint and a cleanup.

It was a beautiful spot, up on a hill beside a crystal-clear stream.

Larry had cracked up a deal with the farmer to paint the house and clean the place up in return for the rent, and if any work on the farm happened by, he would deduct the rent and pay him the balance in cash. It was just the thing for Larry, Josie, and the kids.

Larry got to it and cleaned the place up, everyone tuckin' in, givin' a hand for paintin'.

There was a big flat area of about half an acre where Larry wanted to dig up and put in a big garden, so after gaining permission from the boss, got to and dug it up by hand. He noticed how rich the soil was and after a chat with one o' the workers on the farm, he found it was a spot where a local chook farm dumped chook shit many years before.

The cabbages were huge, broccoli was like cauliflower, and cauliflowers, like pumpkins—a massive production so good that he, Josie, and the kids loaded into the wagon and sold them on the side of the road.

The income they were gettin' was minimal and times were tough in the food department. Josie took the initiative and bought a huge bag o' flour. She was a great cook and knocked up heaps o' scones and made her own bread. This kept 'em goin' for a while but not quite enough to have a healthy diet. The veggie garden was nearly depleted due to the sellin'.

Larry had met a bloke who had given him a bag o' dope seeds so it was into the bush and cultivatin' time was on.

A phone call was all it took for Josie and him to make the decision to move back to Waiuku. His ol' boss wanted him back and offered to pay for the removal costs. Larry wondered about his crop because it was only a matter of a few weeks, and it would be ready.

Viv and Larry headed off early one mornin' to retrieve his crop.

Viv was a wonderful mum; Larry loved her to bits. What other mum would risk things to collect a couple o' pounds o' dope for her son?

The crop was a bumper, and it didn't take Larry long to pull it all and stuff it into a wool fadge.

Just before a small northern town, both were startled by what seemed like a gun shot as a stone slammed into Viv's windscreen.

While they were busy knockin' out the loose pieces on the side o' the road, a cop pulled over to ask the problem, givin' a hand to clean up the glass. Larry and Viv, especially Viv, were beside themselves knowin' what they had in the boot. Viv would talk about that for years to come.

Larry and Josie cruised along with their lives. The job back with the contractin' didn't work out.

Larry managed to get a fishin' license to fish for eels.

He and Josie fished all the small creeks around, while the kids were at school, catchin' heaps.

There was a huge market for eels in Europe, and the price was good.

Larry had a small dinghy for the larger rivers and often fished the lakes abound in the area.

Fyke nets were the go. It had an opening at one end, stretching to a sock at the other. A wing net was attached to the opening, three metres out. Larry fixed the bottom end by way of a stake in the deep part of the stream with the wing up to the bank. Once the eels were trapped, he transferred them to a holding bag and let it into the stream to keep the eels from suffocating until he had finished for the day. Most of the bags held a good sixty kilos. The time was gettin' on, and Josie was to pick the kids up from school. Larry went like hell, gatherin' up all the holdin' bags from the day and rushed to get the kids.

A few months later, after doin' the rounds, Larry found himself back at the same spot whence he had to rush off to get the kids.

What he hadn't realised at the time was that he had left a bag in the stream. It was one of the bags that was full and amongst the eels was one a good two kilos in weight. When he pulled the bag in, to his surprise, there was only one eel in it albeit a monster of a good eight or nine kilos. This bloody eel had nothin' to eat, so finished off all the eels in the bag. This was surely a great example of survival.

Months went by. Josie opened up a small craft shop out on the farm, where they were rentin' a house. The Eels were startin to dwindle, with the run nearly over.

Larry suggested they sell everything, buy a caravan, and head off for an adventure around New Zealand. Of course, Josie jumped at it, and soon they were on their way with three hundred dollars in their kick.

It took a good day and half to reach the ferry at Wellington. The South Island was certainly a beautiful part of the great country of New Zealand.

It took over a year to get to do what they wanted.

For an income, Larry manufactured cane baskets and the like, which he sold on the way. It was a fantastic time they would both cherish forever.

While they had been away, James had got married, Bobby and Len had buggered off to Oz, and young Chad had left school and landed a job as a leky at the steel mill.

Ol' Tom was still at Katrina's and her business was boomin'. Viv and Rupert were havin' their ups and downs. Rupert had turned into a full-blown punter, which was causin' financial difficulties for them both.

Waiuku wasn't the same any more, so Larry and Josie moved to the Waikato where a friend o' the families had a farm house to rent.

Larry got into fencin' and loved the job.

An ol' Maori bloke he had met taught him everything he knew, and soon he was an accomplished fencer. He was a great bloke, Eru, which meant Eric in Maori, teachin' Larry shearin' and crutchin' sheep.

It was a great place!

Katrina got sick of Waiuku and decided she and ol' Tom would go to Waikato to be near Larry and Josie, Josie bein' a mate of Katrina and all.

ol' Tom was hittin' near his seventies now and not really the best o' health. He really would have liked to have got into a war pensioner's apartment, but the waitin' list was long, and they were bein' selective on who they were takin'. Larry was furious as Tom had gone right through the war, bein' one of the first to sign up and the last to leave, a good five year's fightin' for his country!

Katrina looked after ol' Tom. He was good with his grandson and fitted in well.

Josie had a sister in Waiuku, so Larry and she loaded up the wagon with the kids and all and headed off to visit for the weekend. He suggested to Josie that maybe they should call in and check out if ol' Tom would like to come. Josie didn't mind at all.

They stopped for a hamburger before goin' to Katrina's. It was gettin' fairly late, so Larry suggested they give ol' Tom a miss.

After finishin' the hamburgers, Larry kicked the ol' Mark III into life and slowly rolled up to the traffic lights and the road north. He stuck the ol' girl into first gear and let out the clutch. The bloody car started to take off flat out backwards.

'What the fuck was that?' Larry squawked; he couldn't believe it. The bloody car went backwards in first gear, unbelievable! He fiddled with the gear stick. 'No, everything OK.' Josie was just as surprised as him. Luckily, there were no cars behind them. Larry shifted into first gear again and the Mark III soared off. Larry couldn't figure what the hell had happened.

They arrived at Josie's sis's around seven in the evenin', all full o' hellos and welcomes. Josie's sis put the kettle on just to be interrupted by the phone. Larry had made himself comfortable on the couch, Josie beside him.

Larry looked up at Josie's sis. As she walked in, her face was tellin' somethin' was wrong.

'Your father has just died, Larry, he had a massive heart attack and there was nothin' they could do to revive him. Larry sat there numb, as if he'd been struck by lightnin'.

His mind flashed about in turmoil.

'It can't be surely. Was she for real? He was fine the day before.' Ol' Tom had died at 6 p.m.—the exact time the Mark III went in reverse. Larry knew that. He had glanced at the town clock when it happened, and it was exactly six.

Larry felt somethin' inside him. It was a feelin' he could not explain, like he had been hollowed out. He rose up and made for the phone to call his mum. He wished it wasn't true, surely, but after speakin' with Viv, all realty broke loose, and the tears just wouldn't stop. Larry was a fucking mess.

Katrina was there when ol' Tom had a massive attack while bein' rolled out to the ambulance. Both she and her son had seen him die on the street, behind the ambulance, before they could even get him inside.

Larry could never come to terms with it. His dad had died in the street; after all he had been through in the war, he deserved, at least, to die in a comfortable environment.

Ol' Tom was cremated and buried in the war cemetery; at least, he had that honour. All his war buddies and best mates were there to see him off and, as he had requested a hundred times, everyone filed into the bar to have a drink for ol' Tom.

Larry was in tatters. Ol' Tom was more than a dad; he was a mate, and in fact, the whole family was distraught, even Viv absolutely collapsed at the thought the ol' boy wouldn't be around any more. The family had lost its first link.

It took Larry months to get over the loss of ol' Tom.

It wasn't until one day, away, up in the hills, at the back o' a farm, did Tom tell his son to get on with it.

Larry was sittin' in the soft green grass gazin' out over his beautiful country, thinkin' of things he and Tom used to get up to, when he was sure someone had grabbed his arm from behind. He heard ol' Tom's voice whisperin' in his ear, tellin' him to stop all the grievin'.

Larry did just that and said goodbye to his dad.

Larry, Josie, and the kids waded on through their lives. They had always wanted to have a child together. Josie had her tubes tied after her last child, so after a few visits to the hospital, she and Larry were proud parents of little Shane.

Josie had problems with her blood throughout the whole pregnancy; the doctors told her, for her own health, not to have any more children after this one, so Larry made the decision to have a vasectomy.

It was really hard for Larry, but if it meant a choice between them, Larry felt it easier for him than Josie havin' to go through the added trauma of a hysterectomy.

What Larry hadn't realised when he first met Josie was that she had an unbelievable voice. All her life, she had dreamed of bein' a singer in a band.

Larry had a bit to do with that and at one time had bought himself a saxophone. He had lessons by one of the best teachers and had played second tenor in a couple o' big bands. He was bloody hopeless at it, and after battlin' along for a couple o' years, he gave it up.

One thing he was keen on was the bass guitar, so suggested to Josie they form a band.

Josie was thrilled to bits, so they wasted no time in purchasin' some PA equipment and a Bass for Larry.

They had a gig jacked up at the local restaurant. They were a hit, and Josie was soon gettin' a name as a true artist.

They went on to doin' talent quests at one of the local pubs, before expandin' their own talents all around Waikato.

There were a lot of opportunities, back up in Auckland, so they packed up the gear and moved back up the line to the big smoke.

Larry was a good manager and soon had bookings; one o' 'em bein' at a top restaurant venue. He had managed to outdo some o' the top promoters, but it was Josie's voice that had got them through. The money they were earnin' was more than anticipated, attractin' some o' the best musos in the country. Larry's bass playin' was OK but not a match for some o' the top players.

Josie was right in her element, and Larry felt they were beginnin' to drift apart, losin' the bond between them. Josie had never had the breaks Larry had given her and before Larry knew it Josie asked for a separation. Larry understood this and after nearly being together six years, Larry was cut to pieces by Josie's request, but they split up.

Larry continued to visit his son and Josie's kids until one night he dropped by Josie's on the off chance he'd get to see his boy. It was a bad move. Josie had a bloke there and had only been apart for a few weeks. It was obvious that Josie had deceived Larry tellin' him she was concentrating on her music and nothin' else.

CHAPTER NINE

What Next?

The split with Josie knocked Larry's arse in, maybe it was God's way of teachin' him a lesson for bein' such an arse in the past, but Larry had to pick himself up and carried on with it.

He remembered a time he had spoken to ol' Tom about Josie.

Ol' Tom had always liked her but had told his son that she was a woman that was goin' to hurt him one day.

Maybe Larry should have listened to his father's advice the day he shacked up with her, leavin' his son alone whilst he screwed his arse off. Nevertheless Larry carried on.

He moved into a house in Howick with another flatmate, a woman. This was the start of another full on rampage for Larry. It was only a few weeks before he had her in the sack, so moved to another flat in Mt Wellington with another chick.

This one was a bit different, and Larry respected her. He never once tried to swoon her, and they got on well. She even made him cut lunches for work.

Larry got a job as a barman at the local. It was full on with bands playin' there frequently, the place packed to the rafters. It was one o' those places everyone knew of as a pick-up joint, so the presence of available sheilas was evident.

Larry was back to the future, so he thought. He couldn't go wrong with a chick always hangin' around till closin' waitin' for him to knock off and spend the rest o' the evenin' goin' hard.

He bumped into one o' his ol' flames from way back. Carla was a real cutie.

He moved in with her in a boardin' situation, but Carla wanted a commitment from Larry, which he wasn't prepared to give. He wanted a bit o' space to sort out what he was goin' to do. He was headin' into his thirties and things were startin' to play on his mind. He often thought he may be headin' towards some sort of change in his body and mind, male menopause maybe, but nevertheless his future was uncertain.

Larry heard of big money fishin' for crays down the east coast, so let Carla know he was off. Carla was keen to have a change, so tagged along as Larry's partner.

Mahia was a fishin' village out on a peninsula, just south o' Gisborne. Cray boats and longliners were the main fleet with many of them bein' towed to the sea for launchin'. Larry got the odd day with some o' the boys and on one occasion landed a decky job with one o' the best.

Off they steamed out o' the estuary into the open sea. It was a flat, calm mornin', with hardly a ripple. The thirty-five footer ploughin' along at a good seven knots. Pete had been at sea for over thirty-five years and knew what he was up to. Most o' the craypots were out at the sixty-metre mark and after a good steam were comin' alongside the first one.

The grapple flew out over the leader line, Larry pullin' like crazy, hookin' it up, grabbed hold, up and over the pully, round the winch, and up it came.

The pot was chocker block lookin' like a bunch o' 'pick up sticks' as it came aboard. Pete quickly unloaded chuckin' back the ones that were obviously too small and measuring the likelys. Larry swung his arm into the pot with the bait, tied it up, fixed the door shut, and when Pete found the spot, over the side it went and headed for the next one, all takin' around five minutes for the whole procedure.

Pete had over a hundred pots around the area, so it was to take a good five to six hours to get round them all.

Half way through the pick up, Pete felt somethin' wrong as he rounded a pot. There was a good sea run-in by now, and the wind had picked up. The swells were up around four metres. Pete yelled to Larry over the noise of the Fordson that he was pretty sure the pot rope had fouled the prop. This was not a good situation to be in, especially when land was about fifteen miles away.

There was only one thing for it and that was to jump over and cut the line free.

Larry stripped off bollocky and dived over the side. It was cold as ice, his manhood disappearin' into his guts like a turtle retractin' its head.

The water was crystal-clear and had no trouble locatin' and cuttin' the rope free.

Pete gave him a hand back on board, mumblin' about losin' a hundred-dollar pot.

The sea was startin to pick up. Pete had the weather forecast on while Larry was below and informed Larry they were in for a storm. There were around ten more pots to pick up when all of a sudden, the boat ceased to make way. Somehow the day seemed to be doomed—from the start. Upon a visual inspection, Pete found the keyway on the main pulley had sheared.

Larry immediately thought of a dark and stormy night on the high seas.

Pete beckoned to Larry askin' him to lift a hatch near the helm.

To Larry's amazement, there was what seemed like a complete workshop, generator and all.

Pete had the boat up and runnin', but the storm had caught up and soon were on the run to shelter.

The only shelter was in a bay on a small island just off the tip of Mahia peninsula.

By the time they arrived, the seas had beaten them to it and the bay was bein' pounded by seven-foot rollers.

There was only one thing to do and that was to run the gauntlet back to the estuary, the only problem bein' was they would be on a beam sea all the way down the southern side of the peninsula.

The seas were humongous as Pete barrelled the ex tug down the sixteen-metre swells. The heavy rain was obscuring his vision, so asked Larry to take the helm, whilst he polked his eyeballs into the radar.

Larry fought each wave. Down he went, deep into the trough and then climbed back up the sides of the huge swells. What Pete hadn't told him was that the helm was hydraulic, so he only had to steer it as if drivin' a car, but Larry, oblivious to this, was whippin' down the swells fightin' the helm givin' the ship full rudder every time he hit the trough.

It was after ten minutes, Larry barrelled down the mother of all waves, hit the bottom, and the rudder went full to port, swingin' the ship about and broached.

Over it went. Larry could see water rushin' past the windows of the cabin to starb'd. Next thing all hell broke loose as everything in the cabin was on top o' him, includin Pete. Larry tried pushin' Pete off him and managed to bring himself to his feet, lookin' up to face a wall of water so high he couldn't see the crest.

'Fuck me dead,' yelled Pete as he grabbed the helm, throwin' the throttle fully open. Larry looked behind him only to see the stern fully submerged. He had a gut feelin' they were doomed.

The ol' Fordson diesel loved it as it wound up. Luckily, for them, the ship had foundered facin' the huge swells and slowly started climbin' up the face of a wave. Up and over they went and as they ploughed down and up the next, the aft deck washin' free of water and they were away.

'Whew,' gasped Larry, takin' a look at Pete. It was all it took and the pair o' 'em burst out into nervous hysterical laughter. They had been saved by the grace of God. Pete took the helm all the rest o' the way home apologising to Larry for not puttin' him through the paces before they left port at the same time mutterin' that Larry was a bloody Jonah.

Larry never felt frightened throughout the whole ordeal. He kinda knew the Grim Reaper was on his doorstep and so be it, a really strange and unreal feelin', an acceptance of death.

Pete didn't want too many people to know about the ordeal, and they both kept it low profile in the community. Larry fished with Pete for six months.

Carla had enough and headed back up to Auckland, leavin' Larry to fend for himself. He met a solo mum across the road from his pad, who kept him well entertained The Bay was teamin' with paddle crabs. Larry bought himself a four-metre double ender and made a good livin' outta crabbin'.

He chummed up with a Maori bloke, who lived in a shack down the road: no water, dirt floor, and eight kids. The pair o' 'em frequentin' the local, Larry puttin' on the beers as ol' Cougar had fuck all money.

He had not long got outta Jail for robbin' a train, a goods train loaded with booze, but by the time he had thrown off around fifty cases, there was only a crate and a half left. He was caught at the next railway station because he trapped his foot between two cases of beer that had wedged in and couldn't jump off.

Larry left Mahia after a few more months and headed back to Waiuku to Vivs leavin' behind all the crab pots, bins, and the boat and trailer to Cougar. Larry thought he deserved a break.

Larry had a few bob tucked away, so didn't work for a while.

It seemed strange bein' back there without the presence of ol' Tom.

Nothin' seemed the same. Most of the clan that used to be there had moved on with the women they had met, and the ones that had stayed were married.

The pubs still pumped along, but a new group o' youngsters had taken over and Larry felt outta place. He hung about there for a few more months, workin' out at the mill, doin' the drainage for a new stage two. He wandered about the town, sometimes travellin' to Auckland for a bit o' a look around.

Viv was pleased he'd been stayin' with her, helpin' out with a few finances, but Larry was restless. Bobby was livin' in Australia, so thought he'd go there to visit and catch up. He hadn't seen her for a good many years.

CHAPTER TEN

Back to Oz

The jet swooped down over Sydney, the sun sendin' a blindin' flash on the wing as it lined up the runway and landed. Bobby and Katrina were there to meet him. Katrina had enough with New Zealand, and she had gone over a few years earlier. She had met a nice guy and had settled down. It was Katrina's house where Larry was to stay because Bobby had a full house bein' a three beddy. Her two kids had grown somewhat and had a room each. Larry had a room to himself at Katrina's, which worked out well for all.

Bobby, Len, Katrina, and Jed often frequented the footy clubs around their neighbourhood, and this was where all the action was.

The pokies had huge payouts, which attracted heaps o' people.

The whole five o' 'em were there most days from Thursdays till Sundays.

It was here that Larry met a woman the devil himself had sent for him.

Tina was a plain-lookin' woman, never really dressin' to kill: track pants, sloppy joes, or T-shirts and her long brown hair had hardly seen the beauty parlour. Make-up was a complete no-no and thongs were the only footware she owned. At the same time, she was appealin' to Larry and got on like a house on fire. Larry tried to look behind the plainness of Tina. She was a real outdoor type o' woman, never hesitating to knock the shit outta a snake if it threatened, cook up, and eat a goanna, and absolutely loved fishin'. Tina lived in a commission house not far from Katrina's home, so whenever there was an opportunity and the kids were at school, she trundled around to Katrina's with a cask o' white wine under her arm.

Tina had a body to die, which Larry hadn't taken long to notice.

Larry found a job with Len, doin' concrete, formwork, and steel fixin'—a great job that took them all over the city and countryside. Bridge work was a big factor climbin' down into the piers, vibratin' the concrete, pourin' the roadin', tyin' the steel, boxin' up, just a whole array of work.

All the blokes Larry worked with were great. Work wasn't like work, it was more like a big family, all goin' about things in clockwork fashion, laughin' and jokin' and when it came down to serious work, everyone mucked in and got the job done. It was hard work, screedin' concrete, rakin' it back, shovelin' and liftin', but Larry loved it and was in his element.

One o' the boys was a hard case, part Aboriginal. He was fairly tall, his head round, his face squashed in. When he smiled, his mouth stretched from one side o' his face to the other, revealin' a row of falsies that dropped outta his gob every time he spoke.

Larry thought he was a real character and nicknamed him Black Rat because of all the antics he got up to.

Johnno didn't mind his new nickname and would rather be called Black Rat than Johnno.

Lunchtime was usually about an hour, stoppin' only once for the day.

They had long days, ten, maybe, twelve hours. Whenever there was a pub handy, the boys made their way in that direction for a few quickies.

The job was half way through. A pour on the waterfront, where a pump was the only way to get the concrete to it. Larry went like hell beside Black Rat, doin' the screedin'. Len rakin' back and then droppin' behind to finish the edges. Seven blokes in all and a big pour of around two hundred cubic metres.

The pump had literally shit itself blowin' a hydraulic hose beneath the truck. A tight spot to get to and not only that, the hose was a special one, which had to be couriered from Sydney.

It was goin' to be a couple o' hours before the boys could get back into it. A stop end was put in, so there would not be a cold joint in the slab, much to the disgust of the engineer.

There was only one thing to do and as the pub was just over the road, that's where they all headed.

'Seven schooners o' new' blurted Len as they all walked in. The barmaid took one look and knew there was a sesh comin' up.

She was a great sport and, havin' worked in bars all her workin' life, knew how to handle men. A pretty little woman, long black hair tied up at the back, keepin it in place with a thin scarf, slim, with bigger than average boobs for her size, a low-cut top wearin' no bra, so her nipples doin' their best to push through the fabric. She leant over the bar, so the boys could get a real good look at her hooters.

Black Rat's eyes were as big as saucers as he guzzled back his first, tellin' all the boys, 'Drink up, you fellas, my round,' in his broad, Aussie accent.

Half an hour went by and by then, they had done a full round, so it was up to Len to shout once again. The barmaid grabbed four schooners in one hand and filled 'em up. Larry was intrigued by how she could do this with her tiny little hand, and she assured him it came with plenty o' practice.

The next round came about really quickly as the boys acquired the taste of the ice-cold beer.

Black Rat had cornered the barmaid in a deep conversation, his jaws goin' like hell, his teeth jumpin' in and outta his mouth at every word. The barmaid was well aware of what he was up to and humoured him along.

The rest o' the boys were in deep conversation about the job and all really concerned that if the part didn't turn up on time, the job was goin' to be a fuck up.

The next round came again, then again, and by this time, Black Rat was well on the way still gasbaggin' to the barmaid, laughin' and jokin' with her. She was quite amused by the man as now, and then he would burst out with a country music song gazin' into her eyes.

She was crackin' up and when this happened, all the boys turned their attention in his direction, eggin' him on with every chorus.

It was time to go—everyone filin' outta the pub with a bellyful and feelin' the effects o' the beer. They were halfway across the street and noticed Black Rat was still in the bar chattin' up the barmaid. Larry dropped back to get him, but he refused to budge tellin' him he was sure he was in with the barmaid and had decided to stay and reap the benefits.

Larry left him be and caught up with the rest o' the crew.

The fitters had installed the damaged hose, and they were underway again. The concrete hadn't had time to really go off, so they stripped away the stop end and continued on. The foreman enquired as to the whereabouts o' Black Rat, all lettin' him know of his fate with the barmaid. It was a standin' joke with 'em all. An hour later, Black Rat turned up on the job, bloody well blotto.

He could hardly stand up explainin' to 'em all that the barmaid had told him she was married and couldn't make it out after she knocked off.

He coped it big time from all the boys givin' him one hell o' a ribbin'. He was trippin' over gear, knockin' over boxin', bumpin' into blokes, just bein' a bloody cockhead until he finally did a nosedive right into the middle of the finished concrete.

That was it; the boys couldn't cover for him any longer, and he was asked to leave the job.

One o' the blokes was appointed to take him home. The boys all spoke about it at the pub that evenin' laughin' about the misfortune of ol' Black Rat. The next day, Black Rat arrived at work, lookin' very sheepish but really didn't give a fuck.

The club was hummin'; it was raffle night, twenty bucks for twenty draws.

TVs, lawnmowers, fridges, huge meat packs, if anyone could name it, it was probably there. Larry had won a meat pack and felt really pleased with himself sittin' on his stool, the meat pack just fittin' under the table it was so big.

Tina arrived just before the raffles had finished and made her way over to where Larry, Len, Bobby, Katrina, and Jed were sittin'. She pulled up a stool and sat right next to Larry, makin' sure her leg was touchin' his. Larry looked at her and could have sworn she was half cut already but dismissed it as she had only just got there.

They started chattin' away, gettin' on real well. Larry thought she was quite a good sort and had heaps in common. Come closin' it was back to Katrina's and Jeds with a few o' their mates in tow.

By the time it became 3 a.m. Larry was in the sack with Tina.

Larry couldn't get enough o' her as they made love in every position they could. Tina's kids were away for the weekend, the whole three of 'em and when they finally turned up, he was quite surprised. They were a lot elder than he thought, with the eldest bein' eight.

They had been away at their dad's for the weekend.

Larry thought it to be just a lust situation, but as the weeks ticked by, he seemed to just slot into life with Tina. It seemed nothing to him; they were always out, fishin' somewhere or shootin' down the local Saturday arvos when the kids were at their fathers.

Larry set about his job, and life just flowed on by. He was in a comfort zone for the first month until one day he noticed the dark side o' Tina.

She was insanely jealous and whenever a sheila spoke to him for more than just a few words, Tina was whisperin' in his ear how much of a fuckin' arsehole he was. Larry thought really nothin' of it and didn't take a lot o' notice.

A quaint little town just outside o' the city appealed to Larry and would love to be livin' there. It had a population of around five hundred.

The Aussie wildlife was abundant, which Larry thought was amazing. He loved anything to do with nature, always rummaging through the undergrowth to see if he could spot any creepy crawleys, snakes in particular, which this town had plenty. Tina and Larry often drove up there for a look around until one day they found a haven Larry just had to have.

A ramblin', brick, Queenslander-styled house with a covered veranda around two sides. It was plonked on a 100-acre block and for rent. The house was perched up on a hill, overlookin' parched landscape and a decent-sized billabong, surrounded by the great Aussie bush. Roos, goannas, hundreds o' parrots, cockatoos, foxes, just about everything for Larry to get excited about, even a platypus in the creek, which flowed through the property.

He couldn't wait to tell Bobby and Katrina, but to his surprise, they were not at all impressed; in fact, they motioned to Larry if he really knew what he was doin'.

Bobby had had a lot to do with Tina and knew a little about her.

She was trouble. Larry overlooked their advice, packed up Tina and her kids, and headed for the bush.

Larry couldn't believe this spot. He really didn't give a damn about what anyone thought; he had paradise, adventure, and a woman to satisfy him. What more could he want? It was a sleepy little settlement. A store, post office, cop shop, and pub, that was it, the pub full o' the locals. Not many outta towners ventured there; it was off the beaten track. A huge river ran through the town, full o' giant bass, a great fightin' fish, and Larry was dyin' to get stuck into 'em.

He continued to work with Len and the boys, travellin' a good hour to work each way, only a trip to the shop by Aussie standards.

He and Tina ventured out into the bush often, seekin' out giant ants and the like. There were ants by the billions with nests everywhere.

Meat ants or red ants, as the locals knew them by, a ferocious predator that attacked and ate whatever they could kill, cut into pieces and drag off to the nest. A good centimetre long, these ants would even have a go at a human. The worst ones, however, were what the Aussies called a bull ant. About two and a half centimetres long, these were the ultimate of all. Their nests were rarely occupied by more than a few hundred and stood guard over it with vengeance. If one happened to get hold o' you, the mandibles dug into your skin hangin' on while they brought their arse in, inflicting a painful sting. If one scratched the sting spot, it would sting like hell all over again. This could go on for days.

The wild life was truly amazing to Larry and spent most o' his time in the bush.

Larry and Tina had sold his Fairmont V8 and bought a Kombi van only so they could get away to their favourite fishin' spot and camp out in it.

The huge river wound its way from the sea via an inner harbour chocker with fish. Larry had found a spot, which was quite secluded from the hassle of other people. It was further up the river, miles inland from the sea, but still flowed salt water and was tidal. The flathead were abundant here, which were scrumptious to eat.

Mulloway or jewies, as the locals called 'em, were also plentiful.

Larry wanted one of these silver rockets to latch on and give him the fight of his life. These fish grew to over thirty kilos.

The rods were in the water, Tina had just handed Larry a joint, and the pair o' 'em sat back in the sun. Nothin' much was happenin'.

The heat o' the sun was beatin' down on their exposed bodies.

Whenever they were alone there, Tina usually stripped off, wearin' only her bikini bottoms. Larry lyin' back in only a pair o' shorts.

There was hardly a sound apart from the low throb of the Kombi's stereo. Larry gazed down at Tina lyin' there, her little boobs reachin' for the sky. Larry started to stir the more he looked at her mound pressed against her bikini. It was all too much.

Tina was always a willin' partner when it came to a good bonk, so Larry lay beside her, pulled down her bikini, off with his shorts and the pair o' them went like hell until they both exploded and then carried on with soakin' up the sun.

This was what made their relationship; they were compatible in this respect, neither complainin' about whatever. If it was bonk time, it was bonk time.

Larry reached into the Esky and grabbed another beer. He was just about to take a swigg when there, only metres from the river bank, was a huge fin of a shark, slicing through the water at about a knot and a half. Larry jumped to his feet in astonishment. Tina had seen it also as she sat applying sunscreen to her boobs. Larry estimated it to be at least four metres. They found out later that a rouge tiger shark had been hangin' about there for a good couple o' years, playin' havoc with the local crab fishermen. He couldn't believe a shark could be that far up stream, but the fin was the proof in the puddin'.

After all the excitement, they both settled down for another beer and a smoke. With the fishin' rods as stiff as a piece o' bamboo, Larry was gazin' at the tip o' his surfcaster. There was a slight shimmer on the tip, then a little tug, and then nothing. Larry hardly moved, his eyes glued to the tip o' his rod. There was another shimmer and then, whammo! Whatever it was, it was big. The rod bent bloody near double. Larry had made sure he had good tackle and a decent trace because he knew of the Jewies that abounded there.

He lunged at his rod, grabbin' it and worked the drag.

'This fish is fuckin' huge,' yelled Larry as he played the monster.

Tina was racin' about, grabbin' her rod to retract the line outta the water. She was a good fisherwoman and knew exactly what to do.

She clambered for the retrieving net and stood on the bank, waiting for Larry to haul it in. Twenty minutes later, Larry's arms were achin' from playin' the fish. He had not even got it anywhere near the river bank. The fish was gettin' tired but not givin' up, keepin' itself in the deep waters of the channel. It seemed to be having a rest, so Larry took advantage of this and had a spell himself. Larry put a bit more pressure on the line and started to wind it in. The rod ducked once more and off it went the drag, screechin' as it swam out and up the river, Larry holdin' on and crankin' away whenever he could, sweat pissin' down his forehead and into his eyes. Tina didn't want him to lose this fish and spent time moppin' the sweat away.

About an hour later, totally exhausted, Larry cracked open a coldie and gazed down at the twenty-eight kilo jewie. What an awesome lookin fish! Nothin' like he would ever catch back in New Zealand.

He was so excited, he and Tina stayed there in the sun and polished off the rest o' the booze until the sun started to fade. They both crashed out in the back of the Kombi, the jewie all sliced up and on ice in the Esky.

The locals were mainly bushmen, so they thought. Nothin' like the bushmen back home workin' in the dense undergrowth such as the South island offered. Larry clicked with them all, sometimes givin' a hand on weekends in the local sawmill, in the bush behind his house. He joined the local dart club. He and Tina, bein' good players, were always welcome. It was there in that pub Larry found out all about Tina. She was insanely jealous. Larry often wondered why they got on so well with nobody around. They argued every time they got home after a night at the local. She was a real nasty piece o' goods. Larry's mind wasn't copin' with all the stress as he felt he was doin' absolutely nothin' untoward to her; in fact, he was quite happy cruisin' along and not interested in any other woman.

Tina was all he could cope with in bed and completely satisfied.

He was with himself now, but Tina's constant nastiness was gettin' to him. His mind couldn't cope. He thought they were both cruisin' along and gettin' on with it.

His life before had been full o' ups and downs and just wanted to put it all behind him, but Tina wouldn't let him forget the past or the present. All Larry wanted was to settle down with a woman, do things together, and be mates as well as lovers.

Tina was a real wine o' and that was one o' her big problems.

All day long, it was into the cupboard where she kept her flask o' wine.

This explained to Larry why she seemed pissed the night they met at the club, realising the same attitude every night he came home from work. She was an alcoholic.

Larry and Tina had been together, goin' on a couple o' years, the last six months arguing a lot because of Tina's nasty tongue.

One night, after a darts tournament, they had a huge argument; in the end, Larry, hell bent in frustration, threw a glass through a window.

He was more shocked than Tina at the reaction. Larry had never been a violent man towards women; in fact, he was always the pacifier.

It wasn't to be the first time, as a few weeks later, they had another violent argument, with Larry takin' out his frustration, once again, on the contents of the house, smashin' anything that was in his way.

All he wanted was to be happy, but Tina had taken that all away. The local cop turned up. Larry had a couple o' dozen dope plants in the garden, and the copper had seen them through the window.

The following day, the drug squad arrived and arrested Larry for cultivation of an illegal substance. He appeared in court a few weeks later and was sentenced to prison for the cultivation of Marijuana. He was distraught as they led him off outta the court to jail, his whole life in tatters. Tina had done her job well, guided by the devil.

Larry lay on his back on his cell bed, gazin' at the ceiling four metres above him, the walls seeming like they were closin' in on him, bein' only two and a half metres apart. A small window, three metres up and no way wide enough for a man to squeeze through, was the only access to get a glimpse o' daylight. The stainless steel dunny placed at the foot o' the bed, with a basin on the wall opposite. The huge blocks o' stone neatly placed together made up the construction o' the prison, hewn by the prisoners o' mother England. The Pomes.

Larry couldn't get his head about why he had been such a fool by gettin' involved with Tina! He thought she was cruisey but had been very wrong.

It was an early day in prison life. Out for breaky and then locked up again until muster time. It was one of the oldest prisons in Oz, so not at all like the Hilton.

The muster yard was adjacent to the cell block, bordered by a huge stone wall around six metres high. This separated that cell block from the next, each block havin' their own muster yard.

Larry's block was a low-security block bein' one of four.

The other blocks housed the inmates doin' longer lags and separated by the level of their crimes.

In the middle of the yard was a square wall about one metre high and in the middle of that was the dunny.

Whenever anyone wanted to go, the whole crew could see what was goin' on, not at all dignifying to the inmates, but, it was prison.

A lean-to projected out from the cell block where the TV was situated so the boys could watch the odd movie.

Larry soon got to know a few o' the lads and had chummed up with a bloke who was doin', what appeared to be a long lag, for armed robbery.

He was a stocky, thickset chap covered in tattoos. Although Larry had a few himself, Arty's were everywhere. Around his neck was a dotted line with the words 'cut on dotted line,' etched on his skin by way of needle, cotton, and Indian ink, not at all a professional lookin' tat, but, as Larry saw after Arty had showed off his whole body, most o' 'em were home-made, apart from a few nice ones on his arms.

Larry and Arty became good mates chattin' away about anything and everything, at times visitin' each other swappin' books, fags, and the usual items that were available on the inside.

There was somethin' about Arty that Larry wasn't that sure of and as he found out after chattin' to a few o' the other inmates, it was that Arty was 'kingpin' in that particular block. For some reason, he had chosen Larry as his offsider.

The weeks went by; Larry adjusted to prison life. It wasn't as bad as he thought, with most o' 'em there bein' pretty good blokes.

It was a hot sunny day. Larry and Arty had come out to the muster yard for a breather after goin' through all Arty's tattoo designs. Larry had noticed Arty actin' a little strange as they walked over and sat down on the bench seat at the foot o' the six-metre wall.

Arty turned to Larry as he positioned himself next to a bloke, who was a bloody monster. He whispered in Larry's ear, askin' to let him know when the guard in the tower was lookin' the other way.

Larry couldn't for one minute figure what the hell he was up to. The guard turned and faced the other way, Larry giving Arty the nod.

Arty didn't want to check the guard; he was concentratin' on somethin' else.

It was like someone had smashed their fist into a hunk o' meat.

Arty brought his arm up, backwards, so fast, hittin this bloke next to him right, smack bang in the middle o' his face, splittin' his nose open, breaking it instantly. Then another and another until Larry couldn't recognise him. What a fuckin' mess! He slumped forward and fell to the concrete. Arty quickly grabbed Larry by the arm and led him off towards the cell block. It had been a set-up; this bloke had been a threat to Arty. He had heard of a takeover and wasn't havin' a bar o' it and settled it right there and then. Not only that, but there had been a case of a pederphile who had molested a heap o' kids and was convicted and sent to Aussie's top security prison.

Arty settled two scores that day. One was, he was lettin' everyone know he was the Al Uno and not to fuck with him. Second, he wanted to get transferred to the top-security prison to deal with this 'Rock Spider', a name given to pederphiles in prison.

Larry learned the followin' day that Arty was the prison's hit man, a bloke the system had in place to deal with unwanted situations, such as pederphiles. He was transferred.

A few days later, Larry was told Arty had been given sweepin' duty alongside the pederphile. He had snapped his broom handle in half and impaled this bloke, killin' him.

Arty had been inside most of his life, as Larry also found out later, and this was the only life he knew.

Larry was transferred to another minimum-security prison for fear of repercussions from the smashed face bloke for bein' an accomplice.

It felt great to see the outside as the prison bus trundled through the countryside en route his new home.

The new prison was also made up of four blocks, with each housing inmates accordin' to their fate. It wasn't at all like the previous prison in that it was a modern facility surrounded by three fences around five metres high, the outside perimeter bein' mesh with razor wire on the top. The middle fence bein' electrified and the inner fence mesh with the top bent inwards with barbed wire.

The wardens put him through all the usual procedures and led him off to his slot. It was a two-storeyed building constructed in a U shape with the muster yard in the middle. The warden's office and rec room situated at the entrance. Larry's slot wasn't quite as bad as the last one, but all the same a cell and overlooked the courtyard from above.

Larry thought to himself of the days ahead and settled down to get on with it. Early days again, out to muster, and then to the dining block positioned in the middle of the prison complex. The food was not to be sniffed at with good hearty meals and puddin'. Once breaky was over, everyone had a free reign until just before lunch when all had to return to their slots, ready for another muster and roll-call, after which it was back to the dining room for lunch. The same scenario applied for dinner. Back to the cells until lights out at nine for everyone mingling about, chattin' and visitin' their mates in other slots.

Larry's days were spent mainly in the gym, where he met a couple o' Aboriginals, trainin' away at the bench press. A couple o' good blokes who Larry spent most o' his time with, chattin' away about outback Australia and how they lived. Larry was intrigued by all the stories about the Northern Territory, the crocs, snakes, lizards, and hundreds of other animals they spoke about and how they lived.

They also knew the prison system and wised Larry up on what to do and what not to do. He was the only white boy to play league with them when they weren't in the gym.

Larry sat on a small retainin' wall, which held back the grass area in front of the block, chattin' away to his mates. He just happened to be diggin' around in the grass with his fingers and felt somethin' like steel stickin' outta the ground about five centimetres. He let the other guys know what he had found as he dragged out a bread-and-butter knife. Immediately he was told to leave the fuckin' thing there. It had been placed there for a hit on someone so Larry sheepishly pushed it back into the ground, and they all left the scene.

It was just before lights out when Larry was disturbed by a ruckus below in the muster area. It was a fight; one o' the offenders bein' stabbed and dragged off to the prison hospital. It was the same knife Larry had found that had done the damage and was thankful his mates had warned him to leave well alone. If it had been known that Larry had taken the knife, it could have been him bein' dragged off and maybe not a chance of survival.

Although Larry's block was minimum security, there were still a lot o' bad boys there; in fact, some o' 'em doin' time for murder.

Larry took a long drag of his ciggie as he leant over the railin' gazin' down into the courtyard. There were blokes back and forth to different cells doin' trades with books, ciggies, sweets, and sometimes drugs, if they were delivered.

He had just taken a long drag when there went the knuckle on the other side o' the complex. It was Larry's mates havin' a go with a known couple o' troublemakers.

Blows were in all directions some o' 'em landin' in the right spot sendin' the receiver to the ground.

The alarms were wailin' as the wardens belted up the stairs towards the ruckus.

They were too late as one of Larry's mates hurtled his opponent over the rail. It was a sickenin' sound as he hit the concrete three metres below not movin' an inch. The offenders were rounded up and led away as wardens below gathered around the stricken inmate. The fall had been too much, fracturing his skull. He died right there on the concrete.

Larry felt sick inside and just wanted to get the hell outta there.

It had been three months now into a six-month lag. He missed the fishin' and wildlife and of course, bonkin' Tina.

It seemed the whole place was unruly, with no control over the inmates. Larry had witnessed several scraps in the time he had been there, with one bloke gettin' a big hunk o' flesh bitten outta his neck.

Most of the time Larry stuck to himself and just wanted the clock to turn back and start again.

It was OK, come visitin', where the blokes could mingle outside in the visitors' area. Most o' the girlfriends and wives wore long skirts and no knickers. It was hilarious to Larry, seein' all these women sittin' on the guys' knees movin' about so discretely until both their faces screwed up as if in pain as they got rid o' all their dirty water. They weren't the only ones. Tina turned up after observin' her fellow gender wearin' long skirts and had clicked on.

Larry felt the warmth of Tina's pussy as he felt his way to paradise takin' only a few moments before it was all over and back to the chattin'.

He was sure the wardens knew what was goin' on but turned a blind eye.

Tina had changed, Larry thought. Maybe this was an awakening call for her, him bein' locked up. Tina never failed to visit Larry, drivin' more than 100 kilometres each way. Bobby and Len visited a few times, a great time for Larry catchin' up on all the goss.

Walkin' through those gates was the best thing Larry could have hoped for. Tina was waitin' to greet him, givin' him a big smooch before he could say hi. She hadn't forgotten him buyin' a box o' beer for him to guzzle, the ol' Kombi chuggin' along on their way home. That feelin' of freedom was so enthralling to Larry. He swore he'd never be back.

Larry took in the countryside, coppin' a whiff o' the eucalyptus from the great Aussie bush.

They wound their way down the dirt road towards their retreat in the country. The kids were away with their father, so Tina and Larry set to makin' up for the lost time.

Larry had lost his job because of his internment but had managed to get a position, drivin' a backhoe and excavator on a huge project about an hour and half from home. It was a drag gettin' outta bed at four in the mornings to make it in time for work at six. The ol' Kombi bein' a mission to drive the distance, bein' so slow. The traffic was a steady flow with everyone makin' their way home.

The ol' Kombi never missed a beat until he was near on half way home, cruisin' along around eighty kilometres. He thought he was imagining it when he saw smoke billowin' outta the fresh air vents from the motor.

A car overtook him, tootin' his horn like crazy, pointing to the back o' the Kombi. Larry pulled over to check out what the hell was goin' on.

The smoke was by this time thick and black. Larry dashed to the back o' the Kombi and lifted the engine hood. He just managed to get out o' the way as the flames burst out like a flame thrower.

There was nothin' he could do; it was too dangerous fearin' the Kombi would blow up. Larry struggled with the side door in haste to retrieve what he could. His fishin' rods, tools, everything he had for his lifestyle was in there but too hot to get a thing. Cars were pullin' up to give a hand; one bloke speeded off to raise the fire brigade. The flames got bigger and bigger until the whole vehicle was a blazin' inferno, the paint peelin' off the bodywork, tyres burstin' and meltin', the roof bucklin' like a consantina. Larry stood there and watched as his pride and joy burnt to the ground. He was devastated.

Len pulled up a good hour later to pick him up. There was nothin' to salvage from the burnt out shell. The fire brigade had taken over half an hour to get to the scene; by then, it had burnt itself out.

Losin' the Kombi came down heavily on Larry and Tina with no way of gettin' to work. They had some money but not enough to buy anythin' decent. One o' Larry's mates had an ol' XB Falcon; he offered to them for only a few bob, so they were back on track.

A couple o' days later he was back on the job. Back and forth he went, from the early hours o' the mornin', gettin' home around seven at night. There was no time for fishin' and as a result, Tina became bored and was startin' to get back to her ol' ways.

There was hardly a day went by without her cask o' wine, bein' pissed as a chook every night Larry got home. Their life as a couple was diminishing in all departments, with Tina turnin' on the nasties more and more.

Some Sundays were the only reprieve when they all got out to do a bit o' fishin'. Larry decided he'd like to have a cold beer, so they pulled over at a country pub on the way home. One beer led to another and before Larry knew it he was feelin' a little pissed. It was too late for Tina. She was well gone, so Larry started the ol' Ford up and headed for home. He had hardly gone a couple o' kilometres when he heard the dreaded sound o' the siren. The local cop had nothin' better to do but watch the pub for anyone comin' out whose car had been there a while, and Larry was the unlucky one. He was done for, D, U, I, into court and ended up bein' sentenced to periodic detention for twelve months.

That was it for Tina and Larry. Nothin was ever the same again. So after he had finished his time, they split up.

Black Rat's brother had a house alongside a river in a one-horse town closer to the city. No shop for miles but a pub. Pat never lived in this house because he had moved in with his girlfriend. He offered it to Larry, so Larry moved all his gear into it. A big ol' stone house about a hundred and fifty years old, the beauty of it grabbin' Larry in awe! A majestic ol' home, fully furnished!

Larry couldn't believe how lucky he was. He managed to get back his ol' job with Len and the boys and things started to get back to normal for Larry after strugglin' with issues in his life. Pat chummed up with Larry and often turned up to visit with his girlfriend. She was a hard case Aussie sheila who had spent most o' her life drivin' big rigs all over Oz.

Pat had been a big factor for Larry, spendin' time with him helpin' him along with his issues, the two o' 'em sittin' back on the river bank hookin' up giant bass. Pat could see Larry failing in the mental department and pulled him through it.

Larry awoke to a beautiful Sunday mornin', the crows squawkin, magpies yodellin', Galla's talkin' to each other as they flew above the house. He cooked himself up a big feed o' smoked eel, he had prepared the previous night, toast, and a big mug o' coffee.

He was pleased when he saw Pat and his girlfriend pull up. He could see someone in the backseat and thought maybe it was Pat's girlfriend's daughter, but as she opened the door, she was definitely not her daughter. She was a petite little blonde bombshell. Larry wondered what was goin' on as he glanced at Pat. 'I've brought someone around for you to meet, Larry,' were his words, lookin' Larry straight in the eye. He didn't need for Pat to explain another thing as the two girls walked ahead, Pat nudgin' Larry in the ribs. Larry thought she must be at least fifteen years younger than him as he watched her enter the house. Lucy was a platinum blonde, the tiniest little figure, her bum swayin' back and forth as she sidled into the kitchen and sat down.

The morning filtered into the afternoon, the four o' em enjoyin' a few quiet beers and a chat. Lucy was a solo mum, Larry thinkin' to himself, not another one, but they got on great together. She was definitely not the outdoor type but was a refreshin' change for Larry. It had been six months since the split with Tina, so Larry was happy to have a friend he could relate to. Come late arvo, Pat stood up statin' they were headin' home and made his way towards the door. Lucy just sat there lookin' up at Larry with the most come-to-bed look he had seen on a woman's face.

He knew straight away what she was tryin' to tell him, so he bid his farewells to Pat and his girlfriend and re-entered the kitchen where Lucy was sittin'. Larry offered her another drink, askin' her how she was goin' to get home that evenin'. Lucy replied that she didn't intend goin' home till mornin'. Larry had nothin' to do with women since Tina and wasn't goin' to discourage her one bit, and soon, after a few more drinks, they were both stripped naked and hard at it.

This woman was all fired up and gave Larry the ride o' his life, time and time again right into the wee hours o' the mornin'.

He was well and truly fucked.

Lucy and Larry carried on their relationship for nearly a year, Lucy convincing Larry she was a hard out nympho. He knew there would be no future with her as she had issues with her ex, and also, Larry, for once, was defeated utterly in the bedroom. Larry loved his outdoor life and was missin' it terribly.

He broke off the relationship with Lucy, both comin' to a mutual agreement. Larry could feel she was not gettin' enough, and she would have been quite happy with two or three boyfriends at the same time, even in the same bed, thought Larry.

Katrina had gone back to New Zealand a good eighteen months earlier and was back in Oz for a couple o' weeks' holiday. James and young Chad were still in New Zealand. Bobby and Len were all settled. There was nothin' holdin' Larry in Oz any more, besides he was missin' his family, kids, and the good ol' outdoors o' his own country.

Katrina suggested he return with her so they could travel together, and he accepted.

CHAPTER ELEVEN

The West Is the Best

The first thing Larry wanted to do was look up his kids. He had been away for over four years and although he had made attempts to keep in contact, it was fruitless. Their mums had got on with their lives, settlin' down with other men. He was absolutely gutted, but after tryin' to understand everything, he came to the conclusion that maybe their new partners felt that they were bringin' up his kids, so deserved the right of fatherhood. Larry didn't like the thought; he was always lenient towards split marriages and kids. He felt a father had the right to his children no matter what the situation.

After a few phone calls, hassles, and rejections, he decided to leave well alone. Larry felt if his kids wanted to look him up as they got elder, he would love them the same as he loved them then. He let them get on with their lives and he got on with his.

Katrina and Jed had split but still corresponding with each other across the Tasman. Viv, Rupert, and Chad were still grindin' away down in Waiuku. James, his wife Anne, and their two kids had bought themselves a small cottage in south Auckland. He was hard out with his music, his band bein' one of the most popular around. Katrina had bought a small unit in south Auckland, so Larry moved in and boarded with her.

Larry hated the thought of livin' in south Auckland; he would have much rather been out west where he was in his comfort zone but really didn't have a choice.

He floundered about aimlessly wonderin' what he was goin' to do, goin' out to a few clubs and pubs meetin' a few girls, but it was not what he had hoped for until he found a job out west. He was ecstatic.

The Waitakere bush was unbelievable after the sparse landscape of Oz. The musty smell o' the bush waftin' up his nostrils told him where he belonged. Tui's warblin', native pigeons swoopin' down over the blokes workin' away, installin' a new sewer line to service the area. Fantails, grey warblers, wax-eyes, flittin' about amongst a few o' introduced species of bird life. What Larry was thankful of was that there were no creepy crawly poisonous spiders and snakes to look out for. Come smoko he felt really at home lyin' back in the green grass relaxin'.

They were a great bunch o' guys, his work mates, most o' 'em Maori blokes from the Ngati Ngapuhi tribe in the far north.

Come lunchtime, it was a huge cook up by way of a Hangi, a hole dug into the ground where hot rocks were placed below the food, covered with damp sacks and then earth placed on top to cook for a few hours. A few o' the elder Maori's, or elders, had the job o' puttin' down the Hangi startin' it up just after the boys had moved off to their areas to work in the mornin'. It was just as Larry had been bought up as a youngster, havin' been to many a Hangi at his neighbours.

Larry enjoyed the work in the bush and had his own gang made up of James and Katrina's son Bert. Most o' the equipment and materials were flown in by helicopter.

The pipes, bedding, manholes, even the small excavators were stripped down and reassembled once on the job. The rain was frequent, makin' underfoot a quagmire of mud, and the boys found it difficult at times to get about, but everyone was in good spirits, and the job flowed away without a hitch. Come Fridays, they all gathered at the base complex for a few beers. The guitars came out with a few o' the locals droppin' in and joinin' in on the fun.

Bein' right on the beach, a raft race was organised by the locals, so all the boys set about constructin' their challenge. One o' the Maori boys came up with a brainwave to lash together the plastic pipes used on the job, joinin' them together with various fittings, gluin' it into a six-metre waka, or canoe, which all were sure would take the cake.

Larry watched as a few o' the boys slid the raft down the beach and into the water. To everyone's amazement, it actually floated; the four crew climbed aboard, two aside, and started to paddle.

The bloody thing took off like a rocket, the other rafts not even gettin' a look in.

That arvo it was beer everywhere as the boys celebrated their win.

Katrina had been in touch with one o' her best mates from school she hadn't seen for years. Larry knew her from school also and had always been smitten on her as a youngster, but Sue would have nothin' to do with him then, bein' two years her junior.

Larry was nearin' forty and desperately wanted to have a life with someone who he related to. He had been up and down, round about, and was sick of disappointments. He encouraged Katrina to visit Sue as much as possible, hopin' he would get the chance to meet her.

Larry had just finished work, had had a shower, and settled down for a well-earned beer when the phone rang. It was Katrina. She was at Sue's house and informed Larry that Sue was keen to meet him.

Sue was separated and livin' on her own with her young son and elder daughter. Larry didn't waste anytime to throw on his jeans, spruce himself up, and head for Sue's in West Auckland.

Sue had lived out west ever since she was a child and was an absolute true Westy.

Larry couldn't wait to meet her and kept thinkin' all the way there what he was goin' to expect.

Sue had always been a stunner at school, slim and sexy, but all the same, Larry had the butterflies big time. He sat in his truck for a good five minutes before he plucked up the courage to knock on her door.

Larry's mouth dropped open to talk, but nothin' came out.

She was stunning in her skin-tight leotards and skimpy top, her hair absolutely perfect, covering huge round earrings, and her baby-doll face with the most beautiful smile. It took Larry a few seconds to address her greeting as she invited him inside. Katrina was sittin' down, havin' a couple o' rums; Sue made her way to the kitchen, askin' Larry if he would like a beer or rum. As the others were drinkin' rum, Larry decided he'd have a change and accepted the rum.

That night Larry couldn't sleep, thinkin' about Sue. She was perfect. Beautiful, intelligent, loved the outdoors, nothin' like any other he had met in his life and understood Larry. She was everything.

Sue had invited Larry for dinner the followin' weekend, which he accepted immediately. He was nervous thinkin' about the night ahead, wonderin' if Sue saw somethin' in him that he saw in her.

The evenin' couldn't have been better the two o' 'em gettin' along so good Larry knew he had found his soulmate.

They spent the next few months, goin' to the beach, havin' a few drinks together at home, and sometimes goin' to the local. Sue was from the ol' school, so it had been quite a few weeks before anything happened in the bedroom, but when it did, there was nothin' on earth that could take her away from Larry; he was truly in love like nothin' ever before.

It was the first night together in bed, Larry learned Sue had breast cancer resultin' in one of her breasts bein' removed. For the first time in his life, he really learnt to understand women. Sue had the strength of a Trojan as she had to handle the trauma of it all on her own. The most devastatin' thing that could ever happen had happened to her, but she had got on with her life not askin' for any sympathy from anyone. Sue was still on the danger list and under the control of the hospital. Every three months, she was to go there for check-ups, Larry supportin' her all the way.

The months ticked by.

Eventually, Larry moved in with Sue; they were so happy together.

Larry carried on with his job until all came to screamin' halt when the company went broke promptin' Larry to set out on his own again.

He managed to get hold o' a contract, buildin' houses out Glen Eden way but needed a mate to give him a hand. James was tied up with his music, so wasn't available until Larry thought o' one o' the blokes he knew from the bush job. Larry knew a little bit about buildin', but was not a fully fledged builder. He remembered this bloke tellin' him he was a builder, so got in touch with him.

Zac was a real hard case Ngapui. The first time Larry had met him, he was down a manhole, benchin' it up. He popped his head out o' it to reveal a long-haired, bearded Maori fella; his face was covered in black dirt, which made him look even blacker than he already was, his long black beard covered in dirt fallin' down from a mouth completely absent of teeth, his high cheekbones beneath eyes of emerald green.

'Gidday, Larry,' his high-pitched voice was what greeted him as Larry introduced himself. Zac was a real joker, always pullin' pranks on blokes, all in good humour. Zac didn't hesitate when Larry invited him to be a partner statin' he had all the tools necessary to build a house and not to worry about a bloody thing.

It was a split level home they set about to build. The back end o' the site fell away steeply, makin' the rear of the house a good three metres before the floor went down. It seemed months to complete.

Once it was complete, it was into another just up the road. Zac and Larry had a ball workin' together.

It turned out that Zac hadn't had any more experience than Larry when it come to buildin'. Whenever they got stumped on any technical points o' buildin', the two o' 'em called into other buildin' sites after the chippies had gone home to see how to go about tacklin' the situation, laughin' all the way hopin' no one clicked on to 'em.

The next job was fairly straight forward, just a box. The foundation piles had already been rammed, so they went about settin' up the joists and floor. They went like hell to get the job done and, after a week and half, were on to the frame, then pitched the roof, all the time duckin' across the road to check out how the other builders in the area were doin' it. Larry sat his arse down on the back o' the truck, Zac beside it on a bucket. A vehicle pulled up and an Indian bloke made his way up to the site and started snoopin' about. Zac asked of his business there, basically tellin' him to fuck off, but this bloke was irate.

He had walked around the job two or three times scratchin' his head and lettin' Zac know in no uncertain terms that he was the owner and that they had built the house back to front. Larry glanced at Zac and Zac at Larry. Larry saw the look on Zac's face; it wasn't good. Zac argued with the Indian that that's what the plan showed, so that was where the house should be. The Indian stated that the back door was where the front door should be and ordered them to cease work immediately. Larry grabbed the plans, he and Zac peerin' over them time and time again. Zac looked at Larry with his toothless grin; Larry looked at him and burst out laughin'.

What the fuck had happened?

A phone call to the supervisor was all it took. He had acquired a set of plans to set the job out and ram the foundation piles, but the plans had been revised so that the house faced the other way. 'Thank fuck for that,' Larry thought. They were paid extra for the mistake but laughed for weeks about it.

It was so good to be back home where he really belonged, catchin' up on all his ol' schoolmates. He thought how (after bein' away for so long) was it that they all remained out west but realised he had missed out on his youthful years at home. Most o' his mates he had been to school with were well established in business and doin' well apart from a few o' the rebels who were still livin' back in the sixties never to get on with it—in and outta prison for all sorts o' reasons but mainly just gettin' up to mischief. Larry was doin' OK with his business, poppin' into the pub for a few after work, all the boys gatherin' there to yak about the good ol' days and work.

Larry's neighbour was an ol' schoolmate disbelievin' he lived right there beside him.

Chas was a stocky, bearded, hard case that spoke so fast Larry had trouble keepin' up, but he had a boat and mad on fishin'.

The sun hadn't burst through the early mornin' sky as they made their way to the biggest enclosed harbour in the southern hemisphere, Chas blabberin' away about sweet FA. Larry was all geared up for a day out, hopin' for the big one as they launched the boat into the upper reaches of the harbour.

The Kaipara was one o' the most dangerous harbours around, with the dreaded Kaipara bar claimin' many ships over the 150 years or more since the area was occupied by the Pakeha.

The notorious graveyard, the most dangerous with a current exceedin' four knots where the whole of the harbour raced out into the Tasman Sea.

Most o' the harbour was fairly shallow as the lads zoomed out over the sand bars separating the main two channels. Chas suggested they have a crack fishin' on top o' the main sand bar; of course, Larry had to agree, he didn't really have a say as Chas was the skipper. Over the side went the anchor followed by their lines. Chas sat back on his seat and opened his mouth to speak, but Larry got in first, knowin' if he hadn't,

Chas would have gabbled along for at least five minutes before he got a word in. Larry suggested they fish there for a while and then head out to the middle o' the channel. Chas nodded his balding head in agreement, and then, to Larry's surprise, Chas gave an almighty tug on his hand line. 'If he had yanked it any harder and a fish was on, he would have pulled the hook clean outta its mouth,' thought Larry as he felt a little nibble on his hand line. Chas's boat was a fourteen-foot aluminium open type dinghy, with only around 500 centimetres freeboard.

Larry held his line with his arm danglin' over the side, with his hand bein' only a few centimetres from the sea's surface.

Chas gave another almighty yank and quickly started to pull his line in, goin' like hell statin' he had a good fish. It only took a few seconds to get his line to the surface, revealin' a tiny, undersized snapper.

Larry chuckled away to himself, bemused with Chas's enthusiasm.

The time ticked by with only the odd small snapper bein' hooked up, but nothin' decent enough for a feed. Larry felt a good bite, and the fish was on. Bein' only about three metres deep, the good two-kilogram snapper was in the boat in seconds. Chas suddenly hooked up another.

The onslaught o' good pan-sized snapper kept comin' aboard for the next thirty minutes and then nothin, Chas's mouth not for one moment silent, drivin' Larry around the bend. Larry suggested maybe that there were sharks about as the Kaipara was known for its huge sharks and not only that, but a breedin' ground for bronze whaler sharks.

Chas didn't agree at all, sayin' the water, where they were, was far too shallow for big sharks.

Another half hour went by without even a bite when suddenly Chas was up on his feet, pullin' like fuck on his hand line all the time yellin' that he had on a monster, his nylon hand line slippin' through his fingers as he struggled to hang on.

Larry moved up forward to where Chas was positioned at ready with the retrieval net. It was a small shark about a metre and a half long, by the look o' it, Larry thought, a small bronzy.

Chas worked the fish to the side o' the boat, and the line twisted around and around the shark's body. Larry reached over the side, grabbed its tail, and heaved it aboard. In an instant, Chas was up and standin' on the quarter deck as the shark thrashed about bitin' anything it could, makin' a good meal of the fo'ward seat.

Larry looked in amazement at Chas standin' there. He was shakin' like a leaf, tellin' Larry, 'Kill the fuckin' thing, hurry.' It was just another suggestion from Chas that made Larry chuckle.

After everything was sorted, the shark well taken care of, they settled back down. Chas rebaited his line and Larry holdin' on to his. Bang! It nearly pulled Larry into the water as he fought the next shark. They were hookin' up every time the lads put their lines into the water, gettin' near to a total of fifteen. Larry thought it better if they transferred to a different spot, but they were havin' such a ball, haulin' in these small sharks, they decided to stay there a while. Larry's line went dead. He was convinced the sharks had buggered off.

They decided to move. Larry started to pull his line in, but it seemed to be snagged, but he was still able to pull in a bit at a time. It was like he had hooked the bottom o' the ocean when suddenly the line gave way, and Larry pulled in the slack. All of a sudden, he saw the huge grey shape of the monster shark loom up outta the murky water, its head reachin' level with Larry's, its eye lookin' straight at him, turned on the surface right beside the boat, rockin' it about like a cork, slid back into the water, its body bein' the whole length o' it, and then, took up the slack in Larry's line and ping, gone. Larry was in the bottom o' the boat, eyes as big as saucers. He looked at Chas; he was as white as a ghost, mouth open, but nothin' comin' out o' it.

'The mother o' all o' 'em,' Larry said to Chas. He, for once, had the upper hand, conversin' with him. He never replied to Larry; in fact, he never said another word for the rest o' the day.

The followin' weekend Larry and Chas headed off back to the Kaipara for another trip. Same ol', same ol', Chas drivin Larry crazy babblin' on. They had a good day that day, hookin' up some good ten pounders out at the graveyard. Luckily, it was a calm day, just as well because one wouldn't want to be there on a bad one, and they had company with a couple o' blokes in a five-metre tinny. They left Larry and Chas to it and headed off to another spot closer to the boat ramp.

Chas moved the boat into position as he soared into the beach and on to the sand. There was a crowd gathered around a boat on the other side o' the ramp.

Curious, Chas and Larry made their way towards the commotion.

It was the boat that accompanied them at the graveyard. As Larry approached the craft, he noticed a huge dent in the side of it.

All sorts o' people were each vesting their opinion as to the event that led to the dent.

After they had left Larry and Chas, they had headed into a deep channel after kingis. A great white had been seen cruisin' about the boat, gettin' too close for comfort albeit bein' close to six metres long.

The guys on board felt it best if they pulled anchor and moved to a spot fifteen minutes steamin' at twenty knots.

They had been there only ten minutes when bugger me if the shark didn't turn up and started to circle the boat again, only this time it disappeared, then came to the surface, turned, and rammed the boat, nearly tossin' the crew into the water hopin' for an easy meal.

Instantly, they cut the anchor warp and got the fuck outta there. The men on board were really shaken up as Larry could see.

After they had told Larry and Chas what had happened, Larry could see the blood drain from Chas's head startin' from his bald patch.

Chas swore he would never fish the Kaipara again.

Larry and Sue's relationship was on fire. They were so compatible, goin' fishin', picnics, Sunday drives, and movies. Now and then, Sue organised a babysitter for young Tony and the two o' 'em headed out for a night on the town. Auckland had heaps to offer in the entertainment field, so Larry and Sue made the most of it, checkin' out all the bands and clubs.

Sue was still back and forth to hospital havin' her three-monthly check-ups, everything bein' OK. Larry thought it was about time they had a home of their own, so set about lookin' for a property to buy. James had a half-finished spec house he was buildin', so he made arrangements to buy it and finish it off.

It was a great opportunity for them both and set about doin' all the necessary bits to complete the home. It was a small bungalow but big enough for the three o' 'em.

Before they moved in, Larry and Sue were married. Sues daughter had left home and married, so they had a small weddin' and reception at her home.

It was one visit to the hospital that was to change their lives.

After an examination it was found Sue had a lump in her remaining breast. It was devastatin' news for them both. Sue, bein' the absolute figure of strength, took the news on her shoulders. Larry gave her all the support she needed throughout the ordeal. It was a decision Sue had to make whether to have a reconstruction or not. Larry was in limbo land. He had to leave it entirely up to Sue. He tried to understand Sue wanted to try and keep her womanhood, but by not havin' a reconstruction meant only a small operation to remove the breast. On the other hand, it meant a huge operation where they took a muscle from her tummy, pushed it up under her skin, and out where her breast should be to form a new one. It was the reconstruction Sue opted for.

Larry sat in the chair, gazin' at his wife lyin' there, a huge incision from one side of her tummy to the other, her whole body black and blue.

Although it was a horrific operation Larry had to hand it to the surgeons, they were amazing.

Larry could hardly believe how much Sue coped with it all, thinkin' how beautiful his wife was and how strong she was.

He often thought of how he would have been, had it been him that had been through such a huge operation.

Larry also thought of the fear Sue must be having not knowing if all the cancer had been taken out; it was something only she knew, but Sue rarely spoke about it and after it was all over and healed, Sue got on with her life as if nothin' had happened.

They lived in their new home for a good six years before they had an opportunity to buy a house further north on the shores o' the Kaipara Harbour. It was a big block o' land near the sea. Sue was as excited as a school girl goin' on her first date and Larry like a seasoned farmer buyin' a run off. The land was flat with the house perched fifty meters back from the road, a colonial styled home. It wasn't long before they had chickens, a couple o' pigs, and a few calves; it was absolute bliss for them all, Tony right in his element amongst all the animals.

The neighbours were friendly, and Sue got on well with the lady of the house.

It was nearin' mid afternoon. Larry was muckin' about repairin' the pig sty. He could see Sue and Tony approaching him, Sue carryin' somethin' in her arms. It was a little puppy. Larry looked at this black and tan little fella exclaimin' it was a huntaway and should be on a sheep and cattle farm where he could get out and work, but Sue and Tony insisted they keep him, so Larry lost out.

After a couple o' hours, he started to soften up towards him.

He was a gutsy little puppy with an absolute beautiful nature. Larry decided to call him Boogs.

Larry had given up his contractin' business when they left the west but managed to get work on farms in the area cuttin' scrub and firewood.

Boogs was such a good companion and never left Larry's side. He sat up there in the passenger's seat as they roared up the country roads on their way to work, Boogs takin' it all in, especially when they entered the farms Larry worked on. Whenever cattle were present, Boogs pricked up his ears, the instinct of a workin' dog. Sometimes when, on the farm, Larry let him outta the truck so he could run beside it across the paddocks, his big strong legs pushin' him along at an amazing pace. Larry loved his dog and as Boogs got elder, Larry struck up a bond with him that was inseparable, often comin' between him and Sue. Sue and Tony loved Boogs as much as Larry, so the family became four.

The stint up on the Kaipara didn't last as Larry and Sue expected.

Luckily they hadn't sold their old home, so moved back to the west.

Larry got back into his contractin' and ended up buyin' a digger and an old Bedford three tonner. It wasn't the ultimate of diggers but good enough to do the odd bit o' contractin' and drainage around town.

The ol' Beddy didn't stack up to the pressure o' contractin', so Larry decided to sell up and have a crack at somethin' else.

There was a big demand for portable sawmills, and Larry had got wind o' a cracker mill, which he didn't waste time in purchasin'.

Most o' the work was on farms around and about the west and soon had a good rapport with a few o' the locals and got contract cuttin' small blocks o' pines and macrocarpa in the area. Everyone knew when Larry was about because o' Boogs on the back o' the ute barkin' away wherever they went. Back and forth from one side o' the ute to the other he went, bark, bark, bark, relentlessly.

On one occasion Larry had to head north. It was a good three-hour drive, but that didn't stop Boogs from barkin' all the way up and all the way back, even to the extent that he shit on the back o' the ute without even a moment to rest, absolutely drivin' Larry insane, but Larry loved Boogs so much he just chuckled away to himself in amusement. The worst was the clean-up at the end o' it all.

Larry started to achieve good standings in the sawmillin' business and set up a yard, bought a bigger mill, and employed a few workers to help out, but unfortunately, after a few months, the bigger corporate mills slowly edged him outta the market. Luckily for him, he signed up a contract to cut a forest o' pines down the line. After settin' up the mill and orders, he put the business on the market. It wasn't long before he had a buyer, and that was the end o' the sawmillin'.

CHAPTER TWELVE

Mangonui

Since Larry and Sue had arrived back in the big smoke from the Kaipara, things just didn't seem to be pannin' out for them.

After a few beers and a chinwag, Larry and Sue decided to sell up completely and move to the far north. Sue's cancer had gone into remission, and there was no sign of any other activity; in fact, the hospital had put her on a six-month check-up earlier, but now, it was down to twelve months. Sue felt good enough within herself to make the move away and have a life that would be full of fresh air and free of stress.

Their home sold fairly quickly, so off they went to Mongonui, one of the most beautiful spots in the whole of the country.

Land for sale was plentiful, and soon they acquired a block o' land only metres from the beach. It was a big move from Auckland.

Larry hired a box truck, loaded all the gear, and headed north, Boogs sittin' up beside him in the passenger's seat with Sue and Tony comin' up the rear in the family car followed by Sue's daughter and her husband to give a hand.

It didn't take Larry long to get stuck in to build a home.

They had managed to rent a caravan, which they bunked down in until the house was weatherproof enough to move into and finish off.

It was only a modest bungalow, but it was all that Larry and Sue needed.

Larry bought an old Landrover for a getaway beach basher. Sue, Tony, Boogs, and Larry spent most o' their spare time checkin' out all the good tuatua spots and the best places to throw in a line. It wasn't until after a couple o' months had slipped by before they realised they didn't have to go anywhere because it was all there at their doorstep.

Larry and Boogs often wandered up to the end o' the beach for a bit o' fishin' off the rocks.

It was a beautiful mornin, Larry kickin' up the sand as Boogs raced ahead goin' crazy, pickin' up a bit o' driftwood, tossin' it in the air, grabbin' it again, and peltin' back to Larry to throw it into the sea. Boogs wasn't afraid of the water and tore into the surf to fetch it. Larry was so pleased they had moved away to this paradise as he pondered off up the beach every now and then, Boogs heelin' behind him to assure all was well before takin' off again to see what he could sniff out.

The rocks were rugged as Larry and Boogs picked their way towards a point in the distance. Every now and then they come across a small stretch o' sand, which gave them a bit o' relief from rock hoppin'. Larry rounded a huge boulder only to be confronted with a big channel, or gut, which halted their track. The only way around was to climb a shear cliff around three metres to reach a track that circled the gut. Larry was concerned for Boogs and decided to try his luck off the rocks where he was. He was disappointed because where he would have liked to go was the point which jutted out into deeper water, but it was over the other side o' the gut.

Larry set his pack down on the rocks and proceeded to roll a fag.

He struck a light and turned to see where Boogs was, He couldn't bloody well believe it. Here was Boogs half way up the cliff face, tryin' to get to the top. It appeared to Larry that Boogs had read his mind. He grabbed his pack and rod and joined Boogs at the cliff.

Boogs was half-pie stranded about a metre from the top. Larry scrambled up as fast as he could and grabbed him by the scruff o' his neck and heaved him up as he climbed the last little bit. Boogs was all over Larry as he sat at the top, exhausted, lickin' him and rubbin' his head against Larry's. He realised that Boogs was a special dog. He had a lot to do with dogs on various farms he had worked on but had never encountered any dog like Boogs. Larry's love for Boogs grew tenfold at that moment.

They reached the point, the slight swell lazily wallowin' up and over the rocks and back into the crystal waters o' Doubtless Bay. Larry set up his surfcaster, Boogs lyin' beside him, gazin' up at him as if he knew what Larry was doin', almost talkin' with his eyes. Out the line went a good 150 metres. Larry found a good slit in the rocks to prop his rod into, sat back next to Boogs, and waited.

It wasn't long before he noticed a little jiggle on the tip o' his rod and then another. Before he knew it Larry had six good snapper in the sack and decided to head home to cook up a feed for the family.

Walkin' back along the beach with Boogs by his side made Larry appreciate the beauty of New Zealand. The wide open spaces in such close proximity to the big centres. There wasn't a sole on the beach, and it was eight in the mornin', the only sound was the surf and the odd squawk from a seagull. He kept thinkin' over his life and came to the conclusion that he had finally reached the point where he was happy, and he had found the peace he had been searchin' for.

A bark from Boogs pulled Larry out of his daydream, gazin' up at him with a bit o' driftwood in his mouth. Larry turfed it as far up the beach as he could, Boogs running after it like a lion huntin' a wild beast, and the sand goin' in all directions. This was carried on all the way along the beach until they reached the homestead Larry set about guttin' and filletin' the snapper. They were all a good size, one fillet each bein' ample for breaky, the remainder goin' in the fridge for dinner and breaky the next day.

Once Larry had completed the house, he set about lookin' for what work he could find. Bein' the sleepy hollow it was, it was provin' difficult to find.

Larry sat his real estate ticket and was soon sellin' lifestyle blocks and farms in the area. The only thing that Larry was disappointed in was that Boogs had to remain at home, but Sue didn't mind because he was company for her the times Larry was out on the job.

It was an interestin' job. The far north was known for its alternate lifestyle residents as Larry was quick to find out. The majority of his clients were just that and bein' summer, inland from the coast was swelterin' up some of the valleys where most of the cheaper land was. This didn't deter some o' his alternate clients as most of the women literally stripped off completely for the trek about the various blocks Larry introduced them to.

Larry was sometimes tempted to deal to the situation as a man should but stuck to the professionalism of his job. On one occasion, Larry was called out to do an appraisal on a property up one of the valleys. It seemed miles away and after hours of drivin' found the turnoff. It was tucked away up a narrow windin' dirt road, an absolute recluse. Larry parked his car in what appeared to be a driveway and approached the house. It wasn't a house, but just a lean-to constructed of corrugated iron with three sides. In the far corner was a potbelly stove where it was obvious they had made that area the kitchen.

The remainder was open plan with a bed against the back wall unmade. Larry called out, but nobody answered. He made his way around the side o' the lean-to into what appeared to be an orchard, callin' out as he walked through the long grass. It was a hot sunny day and sweat beads were formin' on Larry's forehead. He continued to call out as he made his way to the back o' the property, roundin' a big apple tree only to be confronted by a pair o' legs in the air, a white arse between them and a pair o' balls. There were the owners bonkin' hard out. Larry was totally embarrassed, but the owners just casually told him to hang on a minute, and they would be with him soon. After they had finished, the two o' 'em just got up off the ground, totally starkers, and greeted Larry as if nothin' had happened. Larry could hardly believe it but understood these people didn't give a fuck.

After a few months sellin' farms and lifestyle blocks, Larry confronted the same thing constantly. Not that Larry minded so much, but nobody was buyin' anything and the ol' bank balance was startin' to dwindle. Larry was missin' workin' for a livin' and also missed Boogs taggin' along on the job.

He had struck up a friendship with one o' the local fishermen, who had a flounder quota and had offered Larry a deal flounder fishin'. The only thing that Larry had to do was supply the boat.

He managed to get hold o' a dory from another friend and 500 metres o' flounder nets. No one had fished the area for flounder for more than five years, so Larry was keen to get stuck in.

The first week or two was a trial-and-error time for Larry, checkin' out where the flounder fed the most until he got into a fishin' pattern, soon collecting four to five bins a day.

Boogs loved it standin' up on the bow as they sped along at around twenty knots. It was five in the mornin', the daylight just peekin' through over the horizon. Boogs was up on the bow, Larry aft at the helm. He had just rounded the point when there, right in front o' the boat, was a massive school o' dolphins. Larry noticed the leaders were headin' straight for where he had set his nets. He opened the throttle and tried to head them off. It was shallow water of around one and a half metres where the nets were and the big males were in the lead. As Larry got closer, the leaders must have sensed somethin' because all of a sudden, the sea started to boil. It was the lead bulls; they were roundin' up all the cows and calves to stop them gettin' entangled in the flounder nets Larry had set there. The sea was boilin' at such force from the tails of the big males that it damn near tipped Larry outta his boat.

He had never seen anythin' like it. It was like the wash of a giant ocean liner as it powered up. The whole pod turned and headed back the other way. Larry decided to follow and made his way towards them. Suddenly he was surrounded by at least half a dozen big males right on the surface beside his boat. It seemed like they were in his boat as the freeboard was only around 500 centimetres.

It was as if they were thankin' him for warnin' them of the danger ahead. Larry could see their eyes quite plainly as they rolled on their sides to look at him as he slowly made his way towards the main pod. Boogs was absolutely fascinated by it all.

The water started to become deeper and clearer as they made their way into the channel headin' back out o' the harbour towards the open sea.

The big males had given way to the females and the younger dolphins were all around his boat. Boogs was hangin' right over the side o' the boat, tryin' to make contact with them, the mothers keepin' a close watch as the baby dolphins approached Boogs in curiosity. Larry was spellbound as the young dolphins rolled on their sides alongside the boat to get a good look at Boogs until finally gettin' the courage to reach outta the water as Boogs leant over the side until they finally touched noses. Larry damn near had tears in his eyes at this absolute moving confrontation. Not only one of the dolphins did this, but they all took turns, even to the stage that the mothers joined in. Larry followed the pod right out into the bay until they basically waved goodbye and disappeared. Larry sat there in his boat, with his dog just lookin' down into the blue; Boogs lookin' from side to side to see if he could catch a glimpse, with Larry's arm around his neck.

Larry put back into the bay in disbelief at what he had just experienced, picked up his nets, took the fish to the receiver, and trundled home, all the time in a trance. Larry spoke about that encounter for months with a few people in total disbelief.

Sue was missin' the convenience o' the city. Although she had met a few good friends, she was startin' to get a little scared as to what might happen if her cancer flared up. Larry and Sue had joined the local bowls club not for the bowls so much, but a good social life existed there and a great bunch o' people were members. Sue really enjoyed the bowlin' part o' it but still felt a little weird bein' away from the safety o' Auckland. They had been there for goin' on four years. Larry could understand wholeheartedly how Sue was feelin', so suggested they move back to Auckland. It took them both a long time to decide their fate. They had it all where they were, but Larry felt Sue was probably better off closer to a well-equipped hospital such as Auckland.

They moved back to the west a couple o' months later and left the paradise behind.

CHAPTER THIRTEEN

Trucks 'n' Boats

The trip back to Auckland was one Larry wasn't lookin' forward to, especially in the ol' Landrover. The furniture truck had left earlier with Sue's daughter and hubby givin' a hand, while Sue followed in the car, Larry comin up the rear.

Larry had to give Boogs a sedative because he couldn't cope with the continuous barkin' as he put up with on the trip up. Poor ol' Boogs was like a drunk ol' fool in the back o' the Rover, his bottom lip droopin' like a grizzly bear and his eyes like pissholes in the snow.

Larry didn't feel sorry for him but just chuckled away to himself at the attitude o' him; he was a sight for sore eyes, drugged to the max.

Sue and Larry had sold the home in Mangonui and made a good profit, so decided to buy land in the Waitaks and build another home.

It was a mission for Larry to be on his own. The relentless rain and low cloud hindered the whole operation, but he finally made it and settled down for a life in the clouds. It was a grand home he had built, and he and Sue were rather proud o' it. Two-storeyed, split level, huge double garage, secluded in the bush with views over Auckland to die for. Larry went back to drainage work, tryin' to build his life back up again after the years away. He had lost a few contacts but managed to grab a few more.

James and Ann had been livin' on a fifty-foot yacht and had seen a bargain forty-five footer for sale on the adjacent pier to theirs. He begged Larry to go and have a look, so finally Sue and Larry went and checked it out. It was certainly a majestic lady. A Stewart Camelot stretched to forty-three foot. Every imaginable thing an off shore cruiser should have she had, even right down to a custom-built sailin' dinghy.

Larry fell in love along with Sue. It was an escape and also a substitute for bein' back in the grips o' society. It wasn't long before Larry and Sue were away weekends. Young Tony had moved back to Auckland a couple o' years previously and had started to work.

He had a pad o' his own so looked after Boogs on the weekends Larry and Sue were away.

Up the harbour, Larry pointed this beautiful craft the ol' Ford tickin' away at 1800 revs, pushin her along at around seven knots. Their first stop was one of the many islands that dotted the Hauraki gulf. Although Larry had a bit to do with fishin' boats, he had never been on a yacht before, so everythin' was a new challenge for him. Puttin' up the sails was somethin' he would do once he had a feel for his ship. Their new home had all the comforts one needed to get by, even bloody TV.

Larry was in his element, fiddlin' with all the gadgets onboard: radar, GPS, VHF, EPIRB, fish finder, depth finder, stereo, computer, to name a few. Sue was a keen fisherwoman, so first thing to do whilst anchored in the bay was to drop a line over the side. Fish weren't very abundant in the bays, but Sue was determined to catch one. The line was still in the same spot the followin' mornin' with the bait completely intact, much to her disappointment, but after cookin' up a good breakfast and weighin' anchor, Larry was soon on a spot where they both hauled in good fish.

That first weekend away bought Larry and Sue closer together. The evenings were full of love and lust as they bonked themselves to sleep.

It was like an island escape and as the weeks went by, there was talk of even sailin' offshore to the Pacific Islands.

Whatever the weather, Larry and Sue were off on their boat.

It took Larry a good few weeks to pluck up the courage to hoist the main. He had sailed on the furlin' headsail a few times, but the main was a different story. It was blowin' around ten to fifteen knots, a perfect sailin' breeze, so Larry was told. Up went the main. Larry was ecstatic as the ship slightly heeled, dug its keel in, and took off like a rocket reachin' six knots in no time at all. Larry was yahooin' and yellin', he could feel the power of sail and realised what attracted man to this fantastic experience.

Larry held her course up the harbour and into the open waters o' the gulf. It was somethin' he would never forget, that first sail on his own. Sue was a little apprehensive because o' the heelin' and thought the ship would fall over, but Larry assured her it definitely wouldn't.

The words were hardly outta his mouth when a squall hit them like a steam train, slammin' the side o' the main and knockin' them on to the water at the same time spinnin' her nose around into the wind.

Everythin' that wasn't tied down went everywhere. The look on Sue's face said it all for Larry, and he knew he had fucked it up for ever gettin' to the islands. Sue was so scared she went below and swore she never wanted to sail again, but Larry bein' as he was, soon had her subdued and had many a sail after that. Sue loved the boat but hated Sailin' and was always on to Larry to sell the fuckin' thing and buy a launch.

Work was dryin' up and Larry started to worry. He had commitments with moorin' fees and daily livin' expenses. The buildin' game wasn't good, so they decided they needed to buy a business outside the construction industry.

The first time Larry saw it, he felt he had a winner. It was a huge semi trailer rig of over 500 horsepower. It was like gettin' behind the wheel of a drag car because it had so much torque. A deal was done, and Larry soon found himself thunderin' down the highway on his way to his first long distance delivery, Tom T Hall beltin' out 'Watermelon Wine' on the stereo.

Sue remained at home with Boogs.

She had found a part-time job to keep her occupied on the two or three days Larry was away.

Larry had decided to find his own work with the big rig and moved from company to company, doin' what the truckies call a 'floater'.

There were a few private brokers about whom Larry did a bit o' work for, mainly the Wellington run. Larry loved the trip down in the middle o' the night the sixteen-litre diesel thunderin' along.

It was one o' the biggest horsepower trucks on the road, and when it come to hills, Larry's big rig left most o' the others for dead, down through the Waikato up and on to the central plateau, down through

Taupo and a stop for a feed at Stag Farm, a huge truck stop. It was here all the truckers stopped on their way south for their one-hour drivin' break. A huge meal o' steak, eggs 'n' chips was the main menu. Then off down the desert road the majestic Ruapehu mountain, covered in snow, glistenin' in the moonlight, down the Rangatiki and Taihape, Bulls, and on through Palmerston north, then the trek on down to Wellington, the Kapiti coast as wild as ever in the early winter mornings.

The odd occasion found Larry jumpin' on the ferry to Picton and on down to Christchurch, Dunedin, and Invercargill. Larry wasn't too keen on this trip because it took him away from Sue and Boogs for too long.

There were times Sue went with Larry to Wellington but became bored after a few trips and would much rather stay at home.

It had been a real drag from Dunedin to Picton where Larry waited to board the ferry to Wellington. The weather had turned to shit and the passenger ferries were tied up to sit out the storm.

There was talk among the truckies that the Cook straight was wild and the seas huge. The ferry the trucks travelled on was a private company, so they decided to load up and head off. The talk around was that the skipper was crazy. Larry was very apprehensive about it all and knew how powerful the sea was.

His truck was lashed on to the upper deck on the starboard side, the mooring ropes were released, and off they went up the sounds and out into the Cook straight. Larry stood on the aft deck of the bridge, gazin' at the mountainous seas around the ship. The skipper knew what he was doin' because their course took 'em on a followin' quarter sea so that they weren't bashin' into it rather runnin' with the giant swells. Larry noticed some small specks amongst the swell and realised they were small dolphins followin' the ship as she made her way down the swells. They were the tiny hectors dolphin Larry had been told frequented the straight.

Larry had just managed to fire up a fag in the howlin' wind blastin the ship. He looked out over the ocean at the awe of it, all hardly comin' to grips as to why anyone would be out there in all this mayhem.

He caught a glimpse of something white outta the corner of his eye.

It was nothin' he thought until he saw a bloody small yacht climbin' up outta a trough between two giant swells. What the fuck? He could make out a bloke sittin' back in the cockpit, feet up on the seat opposite him, arm drooped over the tiller, wavin' at him. He must be fuckin' crazy, thought Larry and got even more of a surprise when a woman popped her head outta the cabin and waved at him as well!

Larry was gob smacked. The small yacht disappeared into another huge trough takin' a good minute before it appeared again on the crest of another huge wave. How could anyone have such big balls? amused Larry but respected those two people as true seadogs, who had obviously had a lot o' experience on the sea.

One o' the truckies joined Larry for a fag as they both watched the trucks, includin' Larry's, get swamped in sea water. The truckie had informed Larry some of the seas were up to sixteen metre swells accordin' to the wave metre on the bridge, and at one stage the ship had broached to damn near thirty-five degrees nearly to the brink o' capsize. Larry explained about the yacht he had seen the truckie bein' just as surprised as Larry.

He was glad as they made their way up Wellington harbour to safety.

It felt good gettin' back to the north island. Although the south was beautiful, Larry had a passion for the north and always thought to himself that the north had all that the south had and maybe even more.

He rounded the sharp bend in the middle o' Bulls Township, threw the eighteen speed into second low, and worked the gears all the way through to fourteenth gear as he neared the 100 k sign of the open road. On went the brakes as a young woman stepped out on to the road, wavin' her arms about beckonin' him to stop.

He pulled to the side o' the road the young woman dashin' up and opened the passengers' door. She had a look of fear all over her face, explainin' to Larry that a man had been harassin' her and if he'd mind if she caught a lift with him to Auckland. Of course, Larry agreed.

She was of German descent and bloody gorgeous.

She had been followed from Palmerston north by a creepy bloke in a van and was petrified. Larry dragged her pack into the cab and threw it on to the sleeper behind the front seats. The young lass climbed aboard, and they were off, once again Larry movin through the gears with precision until top gear, which sent them cruisin' around ninety-five kilometres per hour. They were long straights of road, so Larry opted for cruise control so he could have a good chat and a fag with this bombshell who had just got into his truck.

Larry was just over fifty years old. He and Sue had not had much to do in the sex department for a couple o' years. Sue was goin' through menopause and had gone right off things in that area, so Larry was left on the shelf so to speak. Seein' this young thirty-five-year-old reminded Larry that he actually was a man and was findin' her company quite invigoratin'. She stood nearly six foot and her blonde hair fallin' nearly to her waist. Her pure white skin glowed in the midday sun.

She wore a skin-tight T-shirt, her breasts pushin' for all their might against it, tucked into the tightest pair o' jeans coverin' her tiny little arse and long slender legs. She sat back in the passenger seat, so her breasts appeared bigger. Larry noticed she wore no bra.

They chatted away about trivialities, with the young lass always sendin' sexual connotations Larry's way. He was startin' to get the idea when she tried to explain that she had been sleepin' in public toilets, parks, and anywhere she could put her head down.

He knew she was lookin' for a decent bed for the night.

By the time Larry trundled on to the desert road, he was as horny as can be. She had asked if she minded if she could have a quick sleep in the bed, which Larry obliged. As she climbed into the back behind Larry, he looked in the rear-vision mirror as she removed her T shirt. Larry nearly ran off the bloody road as he saw the most perfect tits bob out from under her shirt. She just sat there smilin'. She then removed her jeans to reveal black skimpy panties. Then they were off. Larry could see the mound of her pussy as she lay stretched out behind him. It was too much; he pulled over and dragged the curtains around the windscreen. He kept thinkin' o' Sue as he climbed over the back to the panting lass. Larry could not understand why he was doin' this.

Sue was there in front of him, guilt engulfing him. He could smell the sex oozing from this woman before him, but for some unbeknown reason, he couldn't do it. He lay beside her, caressin' her perfect boobs and feelin' the heat of her pussy. She must have cum more than once in five minutes. Larry was nearly screamin' he wanted it so bad. It had been more than two years since he and Sue had made love, but Larry couldn't carry on with it any longer. Larry's guilt got the better of him.

He quickly reached for his fags the young lass askin' if all was OK. After Larry explained to her how he felt about Sue, she understood and admired him. She felt it would have been a moment of lust for them both and that was all it was, and in her mind Larry would only be lettin' out his frustration.

She remained with Larry for the rest o' the journey givin' him her blessings for him and Sue and said goodbye.

She had been good for Larry. She understood how he felt about Sue's cancer and had helped him through a difficult stage in his life. The thing that amazed Larry is that she never gave him her name.

The whole affair was as if it was meant to be.

Sue was gettin' a bit fed up with Larry goin' away. It had been eighteen months on the road, and even Larry had just about enough, so sold the curtain sider and bought a tippin' body for bulk outs around the city. It was a big mistake. Although the work was there, Larry was havin' trouble, gettin' paid for his work and eventually it paid its toll, and Larry had to get rid o' his truck. He still owed money to the finance, and in the end, his beautiful yacht had to be sold to pay the debt.

CHAPTER FOURTEEN

Larry ended up bloody near broke. He was findin' it hard to get the grips o' it all. Sue had enough o' the bush and wanted out.

Larry felt a little the same way, so they sold up.

He managed a job doin' contract drainage for a big company in Auckland, where the money was regular.

Soon the bank account started to look healthy again. Sue continued with her part-time work and before long, they had a bit o' extra cash and purchased another yacht. Only a thirty-five footer but a little beauty.

They continued on with their lives, Boogs taggin' along with Larry once again right in his element. Boogs was gettin' on in age, and although he was still full o' beans, Larry did notice his hips were startin' to give him a bit o' bother. He was comin' up eleven years old, his hips startin' to give him a bit o' bother, but there was hardly a grey hair on him.

The ten acres Larry and Sue were rentin' had sheep, which Larry tended to in return for cheaper rent, movin' them about from paddock to paddock, crutchin' and even shearin' them. Boogs loved the days he moved them to other paddocks, right in his element, barkin' and movin' them along.

A year went by. Larry and Sue lay back in bed, soakin up the tranquility of the early mornin' in the countryside. Sue turned to Larry with a worried look on her face. Larry sensed there was somethin' wrong.

She explained to him that she had a lump on her neck. Larry felt a cold feelin' come over him. He put his hand where Sue guided it to and sure enough, a bloody lump.

That afternoon, after spendin' time at the doctors, was not a good time.

Sue was petrified to go to the hospital the followin' day.

The doctor had made an appointment for tests.

It was truly a harrowin' time, waitin for the results. It wasn't good; the test came back positive. The cancer had flared up in the lymph glands in her neck; it meant an operation to remove it.

The days up to the operation were so stressful for Larry. He could see the look on Sue's face, and it wasn't good. She was tryin' to be so strong about it all, but Larry knew her and knew she was terrified.

The operation went by without a hitch, the doctors tellin' her all was well and that they had got all of the tumour they could see. Sue was back on the danger list and back and forth to oncology once more for check-ups.

Larry knew of some cheap land back up near the Kaipara. Not a good area, but it meant they could be bloody near freehold if they put a removal home on the block. Larry set about arrangin' a transporter to move a house he had bought in Onehunga. It all went by without a hitch, and soon, he and Sue were paintin' and cleanin' up their new project. It was a comfortable bungalow of two and half bedrooms. Larry had knocked out a few walls and increased the size o' the livin' area. Boogs loved it there and was never away from Larry's side while he mucked about around the property.

Larry hadn't had time to clean up the long grass around the house.

Boogs was sometimes findin' it difficult to get through it because of his hips. They had got relatively worse, and he was sometimes findin' it hard to move quickly, although he was thirteen and still fit.

Larry needed to drive up to the builders supply yard for some bits and pieces. He beckoned Boogs to remain there at the house with Sue as he jumped into his four-wheel drive and did a U turn in the long grass. Boogs was keen to go with Larry and cut across to try and run beside him as he drove out on to the road.

Larry felt a couple o' bumps as he neared the roadside and thought how weird it was as he didn't recall anything lyin' there, which he could run over. He glanced into the rear-vision mirror. It was like the end o' his life. He could see Boogs lyin' in the long grass, tryin' to lift his head. Larry slammed on the brake, leaped outta the truck, and dashed back to where Boogs was lyin', screamin at the top o' his voice to Sue. Boogs lay there, lookin' up at Larry his big brown eyes sayin' it all.

He was pleadin' to Larry to save him. Larry was in a turmoil it was as if he had just run his son over. Boogs was givin' out slight whimpers o' pain as he lifted him up and put into the wagon. The four-wheel drive just didn't seem to go fast enough as they barrelled up the road to the vet. Larry's eyes were full o' tears and panic. The vet placed Boogs on the table to X-ray him for damage. Boogs just kept whimperin' and never took his eyes off Larry for one minute. The vet suggested he keep Boogs overnight to monitor his progress.

Larry couldn't sleep. The tears flowed freely as he awaited the outcome. Sue totally understood how Larry was and how close he was to his dog, but even she couldn't hold back a tear.

The phone rang. It was the vet.

'I'm sorry to tell you, Larry, but Boogs passed away during the night.' Larry could not control it any longer and just broke down. The vet suggested that he go to collect Boogs, or he could cremate him if need be.

Larry wouldn't have a bar of crematin' Boogs and drove up to collect him. He couldn't see where he was drivin' because of the tears. Sue beside him tried to console him. The vet had wrapped Boogs in a blanket and put him in a room on the floor. Seein' this upset Larry even more as Boogs wasn't just a dog he was Larry's soulmate.

Boogs had died from internal bleedin'.

Larry took him up in his arms and carried him out to the wagon.

Sue drove them both home.

Larry couldn't see what he was doin' as he dug Boog's grave in the back corner of their land, wrapped him in silk cloth, placed him in a coffin he had made up, and buried him.

Later, he went to the local nursery and bought a Kowhai tree and planted it on top o' his grave in remembrance to his mate.

Life was terrible for Larry from that day forth. Sue was back and forth to the hospital, with no signs o' the cancer. It was near on six months when Sue started to feel pain in her back. The X-ray showed the cancer had gone to the bone in her spine. It was devastatin' news for everyone and soon Sue was in havin' radiation treatment.

Weeks passed by; Sue's treatment didn't seem to be gettin' anywhere.

She was on to her second lot o' radiation treatment and still no signs of the tests showin' a change.

It was just after dinner when Sue complained of no feelin' in her legs.

Larry noticed she was wobbly on her feet and findin' it difficult to walk.

Larry got straight on to the oncologist at Auckland hospital and was told to get in to the oncology department immediately.

When they arrived, Sue was shown to a room.

The oncologist Larry had spoken to had told him that X-rays were to be taken immediately and that all had been arranged upon her arrival, but the bloody radiologists were on strike, so Sue had to wait until the next day. It was too late. The cancer had spread so fast into her spine she now had spinal cord compression, and there was no chance of an operation to save her from bein' paralysed.

Both Larry and Sue looked at each other, tears wellin' up in their eyes.

Sue would be bound to a wheelchair for the rest o' her life.

Larry gave up his work to care for Sue at home. He did his best to try and cope with it all and reassure Sue everythin' was goin' to be OK. The months went by. Sue's condition deteriorated.

The courses o' chemo were doin' nothin' for her, only that she was losin her hair. Her body was startin' to swell and she soon became incontinent.

Larry had a full-time job carin' for his wife, which went on for many more months. He tried and tried to come to terms with Sue's condition, spendin' a fortune on health foods and mixin' up special diets for her hopin' she would come right. Not only the trips back and forth to the hospital but comin' to terms with seein' his wife go down and down was truly a tryin' time for Larry. It stretched his ability to the absolute maximum, never doubting her strength and their love and stuck to carin' for her no matter what.

Larry was absolutely elated when they were told the blood test had remained the same for the last three months and that the oncologist believed Sue had gone into remission. It was like she had a second chance at life. Sue started to pick up and became quite perky although she was high as a kite on 180 milligrams o' morphine to ease the pain o' her deteriorating spine.

Larry started to make new plans for their future. He really believed and so did Sue that the health food they had religiously adhered to was payin' off.

Sue couldn't sleep with Larry and found it more comfortable on the lounge. It was 3 a.m. when Larry was awakened by Sue callin' out to him. She had terrific pains in her tummy. Larry did his best with massage oil to try and ease the discomfort. Nothin' was workin', so Larry made the decision to call the hospital. They asked him to bring her in immediately. Most of the time Larry managed to lift Sue up into the four-wheel drive, but her pain was too much, so Larry called for the ambulance.

Larry could see the expression on Sue's face and knew there was somethin' really not good although Sue was in good spirits with the morphine.

Upon an examination at the hospital, Larry was confronted with the worst news in his life.

Sue sat up in her bed as the head oncologist spelt it out that the cancer had spread to her liver. Sue looked at Larry and spoke.

'Well,' she said, 'looks like I'm fucked now.' Larry took the oncologist aside to be confronted with news he just dreaded to hear. Sue had only a few days to live. Although he had prepared himself for the worst, it was like he had been hit by a train; there was nothin' he could do.

Larry contacted the family. Everyone was there. Sue was in good spirits actually crackin' jokes to everyone.

Larry absolutely admired and loved his wife; the courage she had was beyond anything anyone could hope to see. Three days later, in the early hours o' the mornin', Sue passed away in Larry's arms.

Printed in Australia
AUOC011448191011
250671AU00001B/1/P